RETURN OF THE BANDIT

Villainous bounty hunter Hume Crawford is well-known for his brutal slayings: he will do anything to get his hands on those he seeks. Out to find and kill the legendary bandit Zococa, despite reports of the good-natured rogue's death, Crawford proceeds to shoot his way across the Mexican border. But he has attracted the attention of Marshal Hal Gunn and his deputy Toby Jones. As Crawford follows Zococa's trail, there are two Texas star riders on his . . .

Books by Roy Patterson
in the Linford Western Library:

THE STAR RIDERS

Dedicated to Alexia Rose

Prologue

There was a deathly quiet along the dry gulch as the tall grey mount responded to its master's bloody spurs and continued up the steep slope towards the sandy ridge. The rider wore a poncho, which hid his deadly guns from prying view. He had also exchanged his Stetson for a wide-brimmed sombrero, but he was not a Mexican. The horseman brought the lathered-up mount to a halt on the very top of the ridge. His eyes studied everything that his high vantage point offered him. A cloudless blue sky in which a merciless sun blazed stretched out above him, but it was what lay below that drew his interest. He swung his right leg over the cantle of his saddle and eased himself down to the ground in one fluid motion.

Every well-practised movement was silent, as if this was not a man dismounting from atop his grey stallion, but rather a ghost. Yet ghosts did not wear gunbelts or carry a repeating rifle on their saddle as did this evil creature. This was no phantom, this was a real man.

A deadly killing machine who hunted wanted outlaws for the bounty on their heads. This was a man who had become far worse than any of the outlaws or bandits he hunted. The poison which grew inside his blackened carcass was like a cancer. It spread throughout him unhindered. What had once been a profession had become an obsession. He no longer killed only those who were wanted dead or alive, now he killed anyone who got in his way. Somewhere along the long trail of his brutal existence he had become one of those sickening creatures who believed he was above the laws that governed all others.

For all the outlaws and bandits he had killed for the reward money on their heads there was one he craved to capture and kill more than any other. The most famed of them all had eluded him for years, and even though it was thought that the bandit had been killed more than twelve months earlier, the bounty hunter refused to believe it. The reward money had never been claimed and that was the one thing that kept the hunter searching for his elusive prey.

The bounty hunter would claim the reward money for the Mexican bandit. It was his. His alone. All he had to do was find him. Find him and kill him.

He tied his reins to a tree branch, drew his Winchester from its scabbard and carefully cocked its mechanism. The sound of the bullet being drawn up from the long tube under the rifle's barrel and slotting in to its chamber filled his ears. His cold eyes looked down from the high dusty ridge at the black-and-white stallion tethered to its grounded saddle.

The bounty hunter raised the rifle up until its wooden stock found the crook of his right shoulder. He stared along the metal barrel, then levelled the rifle until the slumbering man with the sombrero over his face was in his sights.

The hunt had been long. Some had said it was pointless, for there was a rumour that claimed the bandit he sought was already dead.

How could he be dead? Who would kill the most valuable bandit wanted on both sides of the long border and not drag his dead carcass to the nearest law office and claim the small fortune he was worth?

The bounty hunter shook his head.

It was just another rumour like so many others, he thought to himself as his eyes focused through the sights of his rifle. He would never believe it. Only when he had killed the legendary bandit would the rifleman be able to do so.

He edged closer to the rim of the ridge. With each step he kept his sights fixed on the chest of the sleeping man with his sombrero-covered head resting upon the saddle on the ground. The

4

pinto stallion looked nervous as it vainly tried to free itself of the reins that held it in check.

The bounty hunter's finger stroked the trigger of his expensive rifle.

Two outlaws had died at his hands to pay for the handsome if deadly weapon. It was the finest rifle Winchester had ever made and it had never let him down.

A thought briefly flashed through his mind.

Should he call out and give his prey a chance? When he had first started out as a bounty hunter he had done just that. A strange morality had filled his now heartless soul. He had always given them a chance. Then he realized that it was far more profitable just to kill them. Why take risks? He studied what he could see below him. The man was dressed in black, just as it was said the bandit did. The bandit rode a pinto and there was no mistaking the black-and-white horse for anything else. It had to be him, the rifleman thought. It was him.

The tall rifleman closed one eye.

Like an eagle on a high warm thermal he surveyed his victim with emotionless determination. Then his curled finger squeezed on the trigger. A deafening blast shook the hot afternoon air as a red-hot taper tore out of the rifle barrel and cut down from his high vantage point.

The circle of gunsmoke soon drifted away on the afternoon breeze.

Infamous bounty hunter Hume Crawford lowered the rifle at exactly the same moment as he witnessed the sleeping man jerk as his bullet made impact into his chest. Blood exploded and sprayed from the neat hole in the centre of the man's shirt front. Violently awoken, the doomed man vainly tried to rise from the sand.

The bullet had been accurate. Within seconds the body went limp as life escaped from the bullet hole, along with a steady flow of gore. The dead man's horse reared up and tried to race away but the long leather reins tied to the saddle held it in check.

'Got ya.' The bounty hunter gave a nod of satisfaction. He turned and rammed the smoking barrel of his carbine back into its scabbard, then tugged the reins of his own mount free. He led his grey down the slope of loose sand towards the body.

With each step his smile grew wider.

He had finally done it, he kept telling himself.

He had at last killed the most notorious Mexican bandit of them all, just as he had vowed to do years earlier. All those who had said the bandit was already dead would now be proved wrong. They would be forced to eat their words.

The bounty hunter's long strides brought him to the body quickly. Crawford stared down at the blood-soaked shirt of the man, whose sombrero still covered his face. The scarlet evidence of his lethal accuracy glistened in the blazing sunlight. He grunted with sickening amusement.

'Got ya, Zococa!' the bounty hunter gloated. 'At long last I finally got ya. Ain't nobody ever escaped my retribution. I'm the law. I judge and execute all those with paper on their stinking heads.'

He kicked out. His boot toe caught the wide brim of the sombrero and sent it flying between the legs of the skittish pinto. The horse trampled it into fragments within seconds as the bounty hunter stepped closer to his latest victim.

Crawford looked down. In shock he stared at the face of the man he had just killed. Although there were no photographic images on any of the Wanted posters of the bandit, Crawford instantly knew that this could not be the man he had hunted for so long. Whoever this was, the bounty hunter reasoned, it was not the legendary Zococa.

No Mexican had blond hair.

Yet the deadly bounty hunter felt no remorse. All he felt was anger. Once again his prey had somehow escaped. A fury burned inside him like a volcano about to erupt. Crawford raised his right leg and brought his boot down heavily on the face of the dead stranger. The sound of breaking bones filled the air, yet even that outrage did not satisfy him. He glared down at the crushed face of the stranger as the realization festered inside him. His eyes darted around the area as if searching for the bandit he secretly knew was nowhere near this remote place.

Then to his left he heard the sound of spurs. Someone was running towards him. Crawford tilted his head and stared from beneath his own wide-brimmed sombrero at the approaching figure. His eyes narrowed as he studied the wide-shouldered man who was leading his horse towards him.

The man stopped as he saw the body at the bounty hunter's feet. Then he screamed out in horror. 'What have ya done to my brother, ya bastard?'

Crawford dropped his reins, pushed the tails of his long dust coat over the grips of his holstered guns and turned to face the man. There was nothing but burning fury in his hardened features. He squared up to the sturdy man and flexed his fingers.

'Who are you?' Crawford's gravelly voice snarled as both his hands hovered above his guns.

The man continued to approach. It was obvious the closer he got to Crawford that he was nothing more than a cowboy. Yet the man who made his living by killing hardened bandits neither noticed nor cared. To Hume Crawford everyone was a target if they had the courage to face him.

'I'm Tom Coats and that's my kid brother Johnny,' the cowboy answered. 'What ya wanna kill Johnny for? We're only cowboys looking for work. Why'd ya kill him?'

Like a savage beast the bounty hunter lowered his head until his chin touched the knot of his bandanna. His cruel eyes were like that of a mad dog studying something far weaker than itself. They were red and unblinking. Every scrap of his putrid hate had turned on to the unarmed cowboy who still walked towards him.

'Shame ya ain't got bounty on ya heads,' Crawford snarled. His hands dragged his guns from their holsters faster than Coats had ever seen anyone draw before. It would be the last thing the cowboy would ever see.

The bounty hunter cocked his hammers and squeezed his triggers.

The deafening sound of the two guns being fired shook the remote area. Venomous lead spewed from the barrels of Crawford's .45s. Red-hot tapers tore across the distance between the two men.

Crawford watched as the burly Coats was lifted off his feet and sent flying backwards by the impact of the pair of bullets as they found and killed their target. The cowboy crashed heavily on to the sand. His horse broke free and galloped away from its dead master.

There was not one ounce of remorse or guilt in the deadly killer as he studied the innocent cowboys he had just slain for no reason. There was only anger that neither of the Coats brothers had any value.

The smoking six-shooters were returned to their holsters as the man spat. 'Shame you bastards weren't wanted. Now ya just worthless buzzard bait.'

He grabbed his saddle horn, poked a boot into his stirrup and mounted his grey in one silent action. His cruel eyes stared at the pinto standing above the blond-haired body. The bounty hunter shook his head, then spat again.

'Who'd have thought there was more than one pinto nag in this stinking land?' he muttered to himself before turning and staring out towards the sun. Then without a moment's hesitation Crawford drew one of his still smoking guns from its holster again. He cocked the gun's hammer and fired at the handsome black-and-white horse. His bullet hit the horse in the side of its head. Blood splattered across the already stained ground. The pinto crashed down into the sand and rolled over its stricken master. 'Now there's only one pinto stallion in this unholy land and it belongs to the bandit I'm hunting.'

The bounty hunter reloaded the gun and slid it back into its holster. He gathered up his long leathers and sniffed at the air.

'I know ya mighty close coz I can smell ya, Zococa,' he shouted at the top of his lungs. Then he made an ominous prediction. 'And what I can smell, I catch. What I catch, I kill.'

Crawford hauled his reins to the side and then viciously spurred. The animal obeyed the spurs and thundered back up the sandy slope to the ridge.

The hunt was still on.

1

The two horsemen drew rein and stared out into the setting sun. The sky had turned into an ocean of scarlet waves above the men known as star riders. Another day was succumbing to the inevitable coming of night. Marshal Hal Gunn lifted his canteen and slowly unscrewed its stopper as his deputy, Toby Jones, just sat astride his lathered-up gelding and studied the landscape that faced them with young naive eyes. With nightfall came a sudden drop in temperature and the chilling howls of distant coyotes baying to the rising moon. Both men pulled their topcoats off their bedrolls and draped them over their broad shoulders.

They were headed home after three long weeks of visiting every town close to the border within a hundred miles of El Diablo. It had been an uneventful tour of duty for the lawmen yet both knew that out here in the mostly lawless terrain things could change in a heart-beat. Gunn reached across and offered the canteen to his friend and colleague.

'Take a long swallow, Toby,' Gunn said in a tone that sounded as if he were actually giving an order. 'We got us twenty miles before we get home. I don't want to waste any time stopping again to quench our thirst.'

Toby accepted the canteen and took a long swallow of the warm water. It washed the dust from his throat if nothing else. 'Thanks, Marshal.'

Gunn accepted the return of his canteen and gave a sigh. 'I'm getting too old for this kinda work, boy. There comes a time when a man wants to quit giving vermin the chance at shooting at him.'

Toby looked at his partner in stunned surprise at the admission. 'You ain't old, Marshal. Don't go quitting on me before I've learned how to do this damn job right.'

Gunn took a swig from his canteen and savoured the water as it made its way down his throat. He glanced at the youngster. 'There ain't much more I can teach ya, Toby. You happen to be a whole lot better at this job than ya know.'

Toby looked concerned as the red light of the sinking sun was cast across them. It was as though they had both been painted in blood. 'I'd not like to even try and do this damn job without you at my side, Marshal. The deadliest of badmen are feared of you. I'm still looked on as a wet-eared kid by them. I'd not last a week if ya quit.'

The marshal screwed the stopper back on his canteen thoughtfully. 'Then maybe we should both quit.'

'What would I do?' Toby looked alarmed. The only job he had ever had was riding beside the experienced Gunn as his deputy. 'I ain't got nothing except my deputy's wages.'

Hal Gunn hung his canteen on the saddle horn and looked at his young friend. 'Ya could work with me on the ranch. The girls would like that. They're both getting mighty tired of having a husband and pa that's a star rider.'

Toby looked hard at his mentor. 'Are ya sure you want me to work on the ranch?'

The marshal silently thought about the son he had lost less than eighteen months earlier. He smiled. 'Yep. I'm sure, son.'

Both riders pulled up the heads of their grazing horses and looked ahead at the rolling hills that surrounded them on all sides. The shadows lengthened. The sun had disappeared over the horizon and slowly the sky darkened. Twilight was an unnerving time out on the borders. It came slowly and lingered. Stars appeared like diamonds and glistened as the sky itself grew ever blacker. Only the moon gave men like Gunn and Toby any true help to cross the mostly barren terrain at night. Its eerie light was like a beacon and had often betrayed those who attempted to bushwhack the only lawmen within hundreds of miles.

'Are ya set on quitting, Marshal?' Toby asked, his gloved hands toying with his reins.

'I'm considering it, Toby,' Gunn replied and turned his horse. There were no more towns ahead of them to be checked. The next place they would reach was Gunn's remote ranch. 'I figure if we just let these nags have their heads, we'll be home a short while after sunrise. C'mon.'

As the marshal was about to spur he felt his companion's hand grip his arm. Gunn turned and looked at the youngster, but Toby's attention was fixed upon something a few miles away from them on the very top of a high ridge.

'What is it?' Gunn asked as his eyes narrowed.

Toby did not reply. He released his grip on the marshal's arm and pointed to the distant rise. The light of a million stars and a rising moon bathed the rolling hills a few miles from where the star riders rested.

'What ya pointing at, Toby?' Gunn stood in his stirrups and balanced as his eyes focused on the distant ridge. Then he saw him. It was the silhouette of a mounted figure with the moon at his back. The mysterious horseman kept his mount in check and seemed to be staring at the star riders with more than a fair share of curiosity.

'Is that a man, Marshal?' Toby managed to ask as he rubbed his eyes.

'Yep,' Gunn answered. 'A man on a horse.'

There was fear in his voice as Toby asked, 'Is he looking at us?'

The older rider sat back down and bit his lower lip. 'I reckon he is, Toby.'

'Who is he?'

'I ain't sure but one thing's for certain,' Gunn said in a dry, low tone. 'He can't pick us off from there if that's his intention. Not at this distance.'

The deputy was scared. Yet no matter how scared he got Toby Jones knew that

Gunn was always ready to make the right choices for both of them.

'I'm kinda troubled by that *hombre*, Marshal,' Toby admitted. 'Why's he looking at us?'

Gunn checked his guns without uttering a word. He then tapped his spurs and led the pair of them down into a long draw of sand and rock. Both horsemen allowed their mounts to walk at a steady pace as they each kept their eyes fixed on the distant high rise. For a while the figure remained stationary, then he turned his mount and began to move in the same direction as they were heading. He was keeping level with the star riders.

Toby eased his horse close to that of the marshal. He kept squinting up at the rider with the moon behind him.

'He's keeping pace with us, Marshal.'

'I know,' Gunn said as he too watched the horseman who was tracking their every movement.

'What's he want?' Toby asked.

Gunn was thoughtful. The rider was

definitely following them from a safe distance, he told himself. Only someone using a buffalo gun could shoot and hit a target from there.

'Do ya reckon it might be someone hired to kill us, Marshal?' Toby asked as his imagination ran riot inside his young head. 'We sure got a lot of enemies along the border.'

'No gun for hire would show themselves like that critter is doing, boy,' Gunn reasoned. 'Leastways none of the ones I've ever heard about.'

'Maybe he's the kind of man who likes to taunt his victims?' Toby said eagerly. 'I've heard of a few gunfighters who like nothing better than tormenting folks they intend killing. He might be one of that breed. Like a cat and a mouse. We might be the mice in his mind.'

Gunn nodded. 'He might be a real confident killer for all we know, but unless he closes in on us we're out of his rifle range.'

The two horsemen continued along

the dusty draw towards a stream. The marshal pointed at the water.

'We'll fill our canteens there,' Gunn announced. 'Then we'll make camp for the night.'

The young deputy looked away from the rider on the rolling hills far above them. Toby stared in disbelief at Gunn.

'Make camp?' Toby repeated the statement. 'We never stopped to make camp along here before, Marshal. Besides, ya said we was riding on for the ranch a minute back.'

'I've changed my mind.' Gunn gritted his teeth. 'We're stopping here tonight, son. We're making camp and having us a nice big fire to warm our bones and fry up some vittles. I'm tired of eating biscuits. I'm hankering for some of that salt bacon we bought back at Rio Lobo.'

'Eyewash.' Toby snorted. 'Ya don't even like bacon unless Ginny cooks it.'

'I'm the marshal and I want to make camp,' Gunn insisted.

'But why?' Toby questioned. His eyes

darted back and forth desperately between his friend and the rider on the distant ridge. 'Like ya said, we'll be back at ya ranch just after sunup. There ain't no reason for us to stop here or anywhere else.'

Gunn reached out, caught hold of his deputy's bandanna and drew the young head close to his own.

'There is a darn good reason, Toby,' Gunn said.

'There is?'

'Yep.' The marshal released the bandanna and started to pull back on his reins as they drew closer to the fast-flowing stream. 'I wanna try and lure that horseman down here to find out who he is and what he wants with us, Toby. Savvy?'

Toby gulped. 'I savvy.'

2

Seven days earlier, and less than thirty miles away from the star riders across the unmarked border between the southernmost part of Texas and the very top of Mexico, the light of numerous lanterns inside a cantina had glowed out from its windows and doors on to the street of the quiet Mexican village: a village that had no inkling of what was about to destroy the peace it had always enjoyed. Hume Crawford had awaited nightfall before, atop his tall grey stallion, he entered the small village, because the cover of night had always offered him protection. Also, in these parts a gringo always tended to draw attention and sometimes bullets. Crawford knew that a sombrero and poncho became unremarkable to eyes well used to seeing men clad like themselves.

Beaded curtains swayed to the music coming from within the cantina's four adobe walls. A few coloured lanterns hung from the corners of the roof in defiance of the darkness. They also swayed as if trying to lure the undecided into the busy building. A few horses and mules were tied up outside the cantina as their owners filled their bellies with chilli and wine. The fragrant aroma of cooking filled the small remote settlement as night drew on. This was a small village similar to many other small villages dotted along either side of the long border.

As with every Mexican settlement its people only truly came to life once the merciless sun had set. These were a people who lived for the night. They drank, danced and feasted when there was no sun to torment or burn them. The dozen whitewashed adobe buildings had been built to no great design but created where and when they had been needed. The cantina was no different. It rested on flattened ground amid an array of other buildings and looked as though it had always been there. Wild-rose briers covered its walls, yet their fragrant flowers could not compete with the smell of the cooking spices, which filled the evening air.

The sun had set and every living soul within the small settlement was out in the streets going about their nightly rituals.

None of them noticed the horseman who had approached from the eastern edge of the village. Even bathed in the light of a gibbous moon he seemed to be invisible as the grey-tailed stallion was guided across the sand towards the cantina.

The noise of guitars and the melodic voices of men trying to sing filled the village. There was innocence in their voices and their music. None of the men, women or children had any idea who or what was bearing down upon them.

If they'd had any notion, the singing might have stopped. They might have had a chance to find and use their weaponry, but even then it would have been to no avail. This was Hume Crawford who was riding slowly between them. He was no ordinary gringo. He was not a man who could be beaten by normal people with guns.

The bounty hunter hung over the neck of his mount as if he had a bellyache. His wide-brimmed sombrero hid his features as well as any mask. His spurs jangled each time he thrust them back into the scarred flesh of his mount. He, like every other living soul in the village, was drawn to the cantina but, unlike them, it was not hunger or thirst that attracted him.

Crawford was drawn by the thought that one of these people might know the possible whereabouts of the bandit he was hunting. Zococa might even be inside the cantina, the merciless Crawford told himself. It was well known that the bandit was always drawn to where there were females and there were always females of different sorts in cantinas.

Droplets of sweat ran down the face of the bounty hunter as he pondered on the thought that the man he had hunted for so long might be inside the whitewashed walls of the busy building his horse was approaching. He was excited at the possibility of killing again, for few men relished the sickening pleasure of ending life as much as Crawford did. It had become his opiate. There was no way he could or would ever stop.

The brutalized horse obeyed the pain of the spurs and continued on into the heart of the innocent village. It was a heart Crawford intended to break.

The coloured lanterns and lamps illuminated the faces of the people as they relished the coming of another night. It was as if they were all smiling.

Soon that would change.

Soon each and every one of them would realize that the horseman was no ordinary traveller who was just innocently passing through their quiet village en route to somewhere more important. This was a hunter in search of his prey and he would stop at nothing in order to achieve his goal of capturing and killing the man he hunted.

The tall horse was steered through the villagers towards the cantina by its silent master. Unlike the rest of the human moths that were drawn to the aromatic scent of cooking, the rider was not seeking food.

Crawford glanced from beneath the wide brim of his sombrero at each and every face. Then he diverted his attention to each of the saddle horses he passed. Where was the pinto stallion? he asked himself. Where was Zococa's pinto stallion and, more important, where was the bandit? A score of witnesses had told Crawford that they had seen the huge mute Apache, and the bounty hunter knew that where the Indian was to be found, his flamboyant partner would not be far away.

Every clue had led him to the land that fringed the border. Crawford could not understand why he had not yet caught up with his prey. Yet he was positive that he was closing in on Zococa because he had trailed the distinctive hoof tracks of the Apache's unshod mount without ever losing sight of them. It was almost as though Tahoka wanted to be followed, Crawford thought.

The Apache's horse had led him to this small village and the deadly Crawford wondered whether, at long last, he was about to gain his valuable prize.

The bounty hunter moved his right hand beneath the poncho and rested it on the grip of one of his holstered .45s. His index finger curled around its trigger as his thumb rested upon its hammer. He was ready to cock, draw and fire his weapon and kill anyone who got in his way or attempted to slow his progress. Frustration and the sense of failure filled Crawford's heartless soul. He wanted to start shooting at every one of the people he saw smiling.

In his fevered mind he imagined that they were all laughing at him. Mocking his inability to find and destroy the legendary Zococa.

He stopped the tall grey horse beside one of the windows of the cantina and looked into the joyful interior. The horse lowered its head and started to drink from a trough beside the window.

There was no mercy in Crawford's cold eyes. Not even the hint that once he had been a normal man who had never killed anything larger than a fly. That had been before the greed had turned to madness. An unimportant man had long ago discovered that guns gave him power, which he had exploited for all it was worth.

Hume Crawford had travelled on either side of the border for more than half his life. There were no boundaries in his mind. He followed the trails of the outlaws and bandits wanted dead or alive wherever they led. He recognized no man-made borders.

There were no places he was unwilling to go to in order to find and kill the creatures he sought. It was common knowledge that Crawford never gave anyone a chance to surrender. He only brought his prey back when they were dead. Crawford had killed many innocent people to get to those with reward money on their heads, yet he had never once been brought to book for any of his own crimes.

Those who pointed an accusing finger in his direction were soon dispatched to their Maker. Crawford never allowed any witnesses to blacken his already soiled reputation. He had learned years earlier that south of the border it was even easier to kill anyone who got in your way. Hume Crawford knew that there was little law in Mexico to stop him doing exactly what he wanted to do.

Crawford continued to stare with unblinking eyes into the well-illuminated cantina. None of the faces belonged to the bandit he was hunting. Although there were no photographic images of Zococa, the description of him was quite clear.

There were few men who rode, with a massive mute Apache companion, upon a handsome pinto stallion. Even fewer who were left-handed and worth a small fortune to whoever could manage to lay their hands upon him.

Crawford knew that although he had never set eyes on Zococa he would instantly recognize the bandit when he saw him. The rumours that he was dead meant nothing to the bounty hunter. His every blood-spilling instinct told him that Zococa was still alive and Crawford never ignored his instincts.

They had never been wrong.

With blazing eyes Crawford continued to watch the men, women and children inside the busy cantina as they innocently ate, drank and sang.

But where was Zococa? His mind kept asking him the same question over and over again as his eager finger stroked the trigger of the gun hidden beneath his poncho.

Where was he?

He returned his thoughts and attention to the large female cook. She expertly dished up the food that she had prepared and then delivered it to her hungry patrons at the dozen or more tables dotted around the interior of the cantina. She, like every other living soul inside the cantina, was blissfully unaware of the narrowed eyes that were studying them.

The bounty hunter threw his right leg over the neck of his mount and slid to the ground. He dragged his Winchester from the saddle scabbard, angrily pushed its hand guard down, then dragged it back up. A spent casing flew from its magazine as a fresh bullet was slid into its chamber.

Crawford walked away from the grey stallion. He held the rifle across his waist, pushed through the beaded drape and entered the busy cantina.

The bounty hunter paused as the beads swayed behind his broad shoulders.

For a moment none of the people inside the aromatic adobe cantina looked in his direction. Even with a cocked carbine in his hands Crawford remained invisible. The two musicians continued to strum their guitars and sing as everyone else kept on eating and drinking.

The deadly bounty hunter swung the barrel of his rifle in the direction of the guitar players. He squeezed its trigger. A deafening blast rocked the cantina as he cocked and fired his rifle again. Both the guitarists were sent flying off their stools by the impact of the lethal lead. Crimson blood trails covered the white wall. Females and children suddenly screamed out in terror.

Crawford had gained their attention. The screaming filled the air as everyone inside the cantina stared in frozen horror at the rifleman who moved deeper into the heart of the cantina.

The bounty hunter cranked the rifle's mechanism again.

'Where's Zococa?' Crawford snarled as he moved the smoking barrel of his Winchester from one target to another. 'Where's Zococa?'

Several men across the wide room

rose to their feet as though they were going to try and attack the bounty hunter. They were all shot in rapid succession by the deadly marksman before he levelled the barrel of the rifle at the head of a small child seated between her parents. The little girl did not scream. Her large dark eyes innocently stared into Crawford's face.

'Tell me where Zococa is or I'll kill her,' Crawford shouted out in warning.

Few of the people in the remote village could speak or understand English. Only one of those trapped by the bounty hunter inside the cantina had any knowledge of the language. The large female cook moved between the tables, past her stunned and shocked customers, towards Crawford. If she was afraid it did not show.

'I understand you, *señor*,' she said, moving her ample body between the smoking rifle barrel and the bewildered child. 'No more killing.'

Crawford raised his rifle. He pushed the hot steel into her fleshy cleavage above the drawstring of her blouse. He glared into her eyes.

'Where is he?' Crawford asked.

'Zococa is not here, *amigo*,' she replied. 'I know the great Zococa but he has not been seen for a very long time now.'

Crawford pushed the hot barrel of his rifle harder into her tanned flesh. 'Tell me the truth or I'll kill every one of ya. Savvy?'

'I savvy, *amigo*.' The female winced as the heat of the barrel burned her skin but she did not move away. 'He is dead.'

'He ain't dead,' Crawford insisted.

'We have not seen him for more than a year, *amigo*,' she said, tears rolling down her cheeks from her handsome eyes. 'They say the Comancheros killed him. I do not know if it is true or not but he has not been here since we heard the stories of his death. This I swear.'

Crawford kept his finger on his trigger. His eyes burned into her eyes. 'Do you reckon anyone could kill Zococa?'

'No, *amigo*,' she replied honestly. 'I

do not think anyone could kill the great Zococa.'

Crawford inhaled through flared nostrils. 'Would ya protect him?'

'*Sí, amigo.*'

'Are ya protecting him now?'

'No, *amigo.*'

'What about his Injun pal?' Crawford snarled at the busty female in his sights. 'Have ya seen him?'

The expression on the cook's face suddenly altered. She was no liar and could not hide the truth covering her handsome features. She lowered her head and nodded firmly.

'*Sí, señor,*' she said in a shaking tone. 'We have seen Tahoka. Not two days ago he was here. He was alone.'

Crawford smiled. 'Did he ride out alone?'

'*Sí.* He was alone.'

'Which way did he head?' Crawford could feel his juices fermenting inside him. An excitement overwhelmed him.

'North,' she replied, as if she had betrayed a loved one.

'Then I'm heading north.' The bounty hunter stepped back from the female and glanced around the room at the dead and the terrified. Crawford kept walking backwards towards the beaded curtain with the smoking Winchester gripped in his hands.

He paused at the swaying drape.

'If I find out you've been telling me lies I'll be back,' he told the large cook. 'I'll be back to kill every last one of ya.'

Crawford turned and walked out into the moonlight, mounted his horse and rammed his rifle back into its scabbard. His eyes looked to the north. That was where he would find the tracks of the silent Apache's unshod horse, he told himself. Then he would find his true prey. The Indian must be riding to find his companion and who better to find anyone in this barren land than a full-blood Apache warrior? Crawford knew that no one could track like Apaches.

A cruel smile was etched across the brutal killer's face. The Indian did not know it, he thought, but he was going to lead the most ruthless of bounty hunters right to his friend. It would be Tahoka who betrayed his pal.

'Keep searching, Injun,' Crawford grunted with amusement as he held his reins to his chest. 'Ya don't know it but I'm right behind ya sorrowful tail.'

He tugged on his reins, turned the horse away from the adobe cantina and spurred.

The horse obeyed its master.

The bounty hunter rode north out of the village. Crawford knew this land well. There was nowhere for his prey to hide, he told himself. There was no sanctuary from the merciless bounty hunter's wrath. As the grey horse gathered pace Crawford glanced down at the faces of the villagers as he passed. They were no longer smiling.

Now each of those faces was filled with the look of fear.

Crawford glanced down at the moonlit sand and saw the unmistakable hoof tracks that, he was certain, would lead him to his goal. He whipped the tails of his reins across the rump of his grey and the animal responded instantly. Crawford knew that there was another village twenty miles away. Zococa must be there, he thought. All he had to do was follow the tracks left by the huge Apache's horse and the left-handed bandit would be his, Crawford reasoned.

There was no hiding-place. No one had ever managed to escape the most lethal bounty hunter ever to have been spawned.

Zococa was alive, Crawford kept telling himself as his grey stallion gathered pace with every stretch of its long legs. Tahoka was going to him. There was no other reason for the Apache brave to be heading north other than to join his fellow wanted friend.

Nothing else could make Tahoka risk his neck and ride into Texas alone. There were far too many men with stars there who liked nothing better than shooting at Apaches, whether they were wanted or not.

The determined bounty hunter gritted his blackened teeth and spurred even harder. The grey gained speed as its hoofs ate up the dry sand it travelled across. The trail left by the unshod hoofs of the mute warrior's horse was the only thing to have disturbed the sand north of the remote village for weeks and it would lead the hunter of men right to him. The bright moon lit up the trail almost as clearly as a noonday sun could have done.

Zococa was not dead, Crawford kept telling himself with each jab of his bloodstained spurs.

Not yet anyway.

For the moment Zococa was still alive. Soon Crawford would prove it to the entire world. He would become even more notorious as the man who claimed the bounty on Mexico's most famous outlaw.

First he had to find the silent Apache.

The warrior had left a trail that even a blind man could have followed. Then he would find the pinto stallion and then he would pin down and execute Zococa.

The moonlit adobes were now far behind the bounty hunter but the blood he had spilled there had still not had time to dry. How many more innocents would Crawford kill before he could get the bandit in his gun sights? The bounty hunter glanced back at the tiny village and spat.

Only the dust from his horse's hoofs and the haunting sound of grief remained as evidence that he had ever been there at all.

That and the bodies he had slain in the now silent cantina.

Hume Crawford forged on.

3

It had taken two days of hard riding for the bounty hunter to navigate the continuously changing landscape before he had reached the outskirts of the town known as Rio Cortez. The horseman reined in and looked down at the large settlement stretched out before his sand-filled eyes. Crawford had followed the solitary tracks of the unshod horse for almost twenty miles. They had led him to the sandy bluff and continued on across the pristine dunes to the whitewashed adobes.

The town was bathed in the rays of the merciless sun. Crawford had never known it to be hotter. The skin of his face was caked in dust and dried sweat. Only the brim of his sombrero prevented it from being burned off his bones. Again he checked his holstered guns beneath his poncho with skilled fingers, which could load the weapons without him ever having to cast his eyes upon them. He was like a killing machine that had long ceased to have the faults all normal men are cursed with.

Crawford had become nothing more than a creature who destroyed all other creatures with heartless precision. There was not an ounce of humanity left in him. Once he had been driven by greed; he had wanted the bounty money on the heads of the most valuable outlaws and bandits and he defied the risks that those dangerous enterprises entailed. Then, when he had more money than he could ever spend in his lifetime Crawford became driven by another, more pressing desire.

He simply wanted to kill.

It was an act in which he had grown expert. The sheer lust of being able to destroy anything or anyone he aimed his weaponry at had become his only true mistress.

They say that all men require a drug in order to continue living. Most turned to the whiskey bottle or just indulged in one cigar after another until their lungs no longer worked, but for Crawford his drug was being the bringer of death itself.

It had become instinctive. It was his only reason to exist. Yet for all those he had hunted and killed there was one wanted man that Crawford desired to capture and kill more than any other.

The legendary Zococa.

Had he the power to do so? Crawford would have willingly allowed all of his other victims to be brought back to life just to have that one notch on his gun grip: to be the man who bested Zococa.

Hundreds of men had vainly tried to get the better of the young bandit but none had ever managed to get close to achieving their goal.

For years Crawford had vainly tried to find the bandit known as Zococa and then, when he thought he was closer than he had ever been before, he heard the news that the devilish Comancheros had robbed him of his prize. The stories of the outlaw's death had spread like a wildfire throughout the lands above and below the border.

It had seemed that the one true trophy that could have etched Crawford's name in the bloodstained history of the West was lost to the infamous bounty hunter.

Then he had heard whispers that although severely wounded the famed left-handed bandit was not dead at all. His massive Apache companion had taken him away. Tahoka had secreted Zococa somewhere to have the bullets cut from his flesh and allow his body time to fully heal.

The whispers had become deafening, like the hissing of a thousand sidewinders. They filled the mind of the bounty hunter with renewed desire to fulfil his deadly ambition.

Crawford had started his hunt once again. This time he would not allow anyone else to steal his thunder and snatch his prey from his grasp.

Zococa was his. His alone.

It was noon and heat haze was rising

from the sand like a shimmering screen of gauze. It blurred the settlement to the narrowed eyes of the hunter but he knew the huge Apache had ridden into Rio Cortez only a day or so ahead of him.

Perhaps he was still there.

Maybe he was there with Zococa.

Crawford rammed his spurs into the flanks of his grey stallion and drove it forward towards the town. For days he had not fed or watered his mount. He had not allowed the exhausted animal to rest for even a heartbeat. There was an unholy urgency in Crawford now. He could smell his prey somewhere close. The Apache had led him to a town close to the border and Crawford wanted nothing more than to destroy both of the bandits before they crossed over into Texas.

There was only one thought in his mind as he forced the stallion with the grey tail past the first of the town's white buildings.

He had to find Tahoka quickly.

Find him before he fled again. Every nerve of the rider's body felt that he was close. Was he with his companion? So many questions burned through Crawford's rancid brain and there came not a solitary answer.

The horse somehow defied its own pain and thundered through the winding streets until it reached the very centre of the sprawling settlement. With the sun almost directly overhead there were few shadows. There were even fewer people on the streets.

The bounty hunter eased back on his reins and slowed his sweating mount as his eyes darted all around the central part of the town.

A dozen assorted types of businesses were spread out around a dry fountain. As in so many other similar towns south of the border, they were all shuttered and closed. The horseman had known that only when darkness returned would the activity resume.

The town appeared to be deserted. Only two cantinas, situated directly opposite one another, showed any hint of life. A few burros were tied up to hitching poles around the area, but there was no sign of any horses. Crawford had lost the trail of tracks he had followed to Rio Cortez as soon as he had entered the settlement. The ground was churned up throughout the town. Crawford held his horse in check as he balanced in his stirrups and continued to survey everything in sight.

As with all men of his profession Crawford knew that the least likely place a gunman could shoot from was usually where deadly gunfire would come from. If the huge Apache warrior even suspected he was being followed by a bounty hunter, Crawford realized that he might choose to end the chase with a well-placed bullet.

The horseman's eyes kept searching for trouble, but there was none.

The only trouble which might disrupt the tranquil Rio Cortez would more than likely come from Crawford himself. He left bodies behind him the way most men left cigar butts.

Crawford rode around the fountain and studied both the cantinas like a hawk watching its next victim. He kneed the horse to approach one of them, then swiftly dismounted. The horse walked away from its brutal master to a trough and started to drink.

The bounty hunter strode across the sand to the beaded curtain of the nearer of the cantinas. The smell of strong coffee and stale tobacco smoke filled his nostrils. With one hand on one of his holstered guns he pulled the beads apart and glared inside the small interior. Two men, more asleep than awake, turned their heads and looked at the tall stranger. Neither of them showed any interest and returned their attention to their drinks.

Crawford released the beaded curtain and turned round. His eyes burned like branding-irons on the other cantina across the wide street. His spurs rang out a menacing tune as he walked around the dust-filled fountain towards the identical curtain of swaying beads.

With each step Crawford felt as if he was getting closer to his prey. The hairs on his neck began to tingle as though they were sensing something he had yet to fully comprehend.

He paused.

His eyes noticed the narrow alley that ran along the side of the cantina, leading to the rear of the building. The whitewashed walls had made it virtually invisible to his tired eyes when he had been astride his grey. The sun glared off the walls as if trying to blind the bounty hunter.

Curiously, Crawford walked towards the alley. As he entered it he could see where horses had left their mark as their saddles had scraped the wash from the adobe. His spurs seemed to grow louder in the confines of the alley.

No wonder there were no horses out in the street, Crawford thought. If there were any they were always led to the rear of the building.

The bounty hunter reached the back

of the cantina. Again he stopped. He studied the large courtyard and then saw the tracks of the unshod horse leading straight across its sand to a small stable. Like everything else in Rio Cortez it was made of adobe and had been painted white.

The deadly hunter knelt and stared at the tracks.

Crawford had followed them for so long that he knew them better than he knew the backs of his own hands. There was no doubt that these were the hoof tracks of the Apache's horse, he told himself. He rose back up and drew his .45s with silent anticipation. His every instinct had told him that Tahoka was near.

Without taking his eyes off the rear door of the cantina Crawford walked in the hoof marks to the stable. He rested his back against the wall close to the open doorway, turned and peered inside its interior. He had wanted there to be two horses stabled inside the adobe, but there was only one.

Crawford cocked his gun hammers.

There was no sign of the pinto stallion. Only the black unshod horse that the warrior rode was there. Its saddle hung over a waist-high wooden wall. Crawford approached it. He looked at it and gave a knowing nod before he spun on his heels and retraced his footsteps. He emerged back into the blinding sunshine and stopped.

A pair of doves flew unexpectedly from the corner to his left. They passed within inches of the tall bounty hunter, causing him to twist on his heels.

Then he saw the towering figure of Tahoka. The massive mute Apache had just stepped from the cantina as if he was going to check on his horse.

For what seemed like an eternity to both men they stared at one another in startled disbelief. It was the deadly bounty hunter who reacted first. Crawford raised his guns, aimed and then pulled on their triggers.

The sound of the guns firing echoed around the courtyard.

Two bullets exploded from the barrels of Crawford's six-shooters. Faster than the gunman thought possible the huge brave threw his hefty frame back into the cantina as the bullets hit the wall, sending dust spewing from the scarred adobe. Instantly Crawford cocked and fired both his .45s again.

Two more massive chunks were blown from the wall near the rear door of the cantina. Crawford could not believe that he had missed his target, for there had been few larger ones that he had ever shot at before.

'Get back here!' the bounty hunter yelled out as his thumbs clawed on his hammers once more. Without even thinking the deadly gunman chased his prey into the cantina. He had no sooner entered than a bullet ripped through the air and tore his sombrero from his head. He ducked and blindly fired both his guns once again.

Another shot rang out from across the long room. Tahoka had found his rifle and was using it to fend off his attacker. Crawford screwed up his eyes and stared through the choking gun-smoke. He could just make out a shadow on a wall. It showed that the massive Apache had his Winchester in his hands and was crouched beside an upturned chair.

The beaded curtain swayed behind Tahoka as proof that the few people who had been inside the cantina had fled.

Crawford had felt the heat of the bullet as it passed within inches of his face. He was now angry because one of his chosen targets had the guts to return fire. The lethal destroyer of life had grown used to killing people who were either unarmed or had their backs to him.

Few, if any, had ever had the chance to fight back. Tahoka was a warrior and was fighting back. It was unnerving to the bounty hunter.

This was not the way he had planned his confrontation with the man he had hunted. A thought flashed through

Crawford's mind. If Tahoka was willing to fight for his life how far would his more famous partner go to defend himself? Another volley of shots came from Tahoka's rifle. Chunks of whitewashed debris fell from the holes in the wall behind the crouching Crawford.

The bounty hunter dragged a table from a wall and turned it on to its edge. No sooner had he huddled down behind it than two massive holes were blasted through its wooden top.

A million splinters showered over the bounty hunter. This was a fight and he was not used to fighting. He was used to executing his victims. Suddenly Crawford began to realize that he had a battle on his hands.

A battle he might not be able to win.

He felt the table rock as another bullet tore through it just to his side. He grabbed one of the table's legs and hauled it across the tiled floor until he was close to another. Crawford kicked the second table over on to its side so that he had two wooden obstacles between himself and the Apache's bullets.

He holstered one of his guns and shook the spent casings from the other. He reloaded with fresh bullets from his gunbelt.

As he snapped the gun's chamber into the body of the .45 he heard movement. Tahoka was making a break.

Crawford crawled round the side of the upturned tables and caught a glimpse of the massive Indian as he escaped into the blinding sunlight. The Apache fired his Winchester as he dived out through the curtain of beads. The bounty hunter saw the huge man roll over on the sand and then start running again.

'Damn it all!' Crawford scrambled up on to his boot leather and raced across the cantina to the swaying beaded curtain. He cautiously edged out of the cantina into the street. There was no sight of Tahoka himself but the dust his running feet had disturbed still hung in the air. 'Hell! He's headed back to his horse.'

Crawford turned and ran back through the smoke-filled cantina towards the rear doorway. No sooner had he reached it than he saw the Apache crossing the courtyard back to the stable and his horse.

For a man of his huge size Tahoka could run faster than anyone Crawford had ever seen. The brave had almost reached the stable as the bounty hunter fanned his gun hammer three times. He saw one of his bullets knock the Apache out of his stride. The large man tumbled into the stable.

Crawford rubbed his mouth on his sleeve. 'Ha! I got ya with one of them shots, Injun.'

Tahoka had hit the floor inside the stable hard. His rifle had fallen from his huge hands. He grunted, crawled to his Winchester and snatched it up off the sand. Then, as he forced himself up he suddenly realized why he had been punched off his feet. Any normal-sized man would have been doubled up in agony, but not the huge Apache brave.

He had experienced far worse pain than that which nagged at his chest and shoulder. When a man has been tortured and brought to the very brink of death itself, he tends not to recognize wounds as quickly as most men. Tahoka ran fingers across his chest and stared at the blood on them.

He had been shot.

His hooded eyes narrowed. He stared at the blood that ran freely from the bullet hole just under his collarbone. A fury boiled inside the big man's breast.

Tahoka cranked the mechanism of the rifle and looked through the gap between the door and its frame. He could see the bounty hunter by the cantina's rear door.

The Apache swiftly raised his rifle and fired.

He saw Crawford take cover. Tahoka cocked his Winchester again and sent another bullet tearing through the dry air towards the bounty hunter. This time his shot came closer. He watched the man back away into the relative gloom of the cantina.

Then, ignoring his own pain, Tahoka rested the rifle against the wall of the stable and rushed to his horse. He grabbed a blanket off the wooden partition and laid it across the black horse's back. He then snatched his saddle and threw it over the blanket. He reached under the belly of his horse and grabbed the cinch strap. Within no more than a minute the large warrior had readied his horse. He placed a hand on the nose of the black as if calming the nervous animal, then returned to his rifle.

He picked the weapon up, cranked its hand guard and again looked through the gap between the door and the frame at the ruthless bounty hunter.

Crawford was still inside the cantina, using its sturdy walls to protect him.

Tahoka focused like an eagle on the face of the bounty hunter forty feet away from him. He knew exactly who the man who had been hunting him was, and he had been deliberately leading him away from Zococa.

Blood was spitting from the wound in his chest as he levelled his rifle up to his other shoulder and stared along its gleaming barrel. Crimson gore was soaking his buckskin shirt and his heart pounded like a war drum.

Every inch of him wanted to kill Crawford the way he knew the sickening bounty hunter had killed so many others. Yet Tahoka had never killed anyone in cold blood. Unlike so many other men in the wilds of the West, Tahoka only killed when there was no alternative. He thought about how he had learned of the deadly bounty hunter who had unknowingly come within a half-mile of the wounded Zococa. It had been then that the Apache had decided to lead Crawford as far away from his friend as possible.

Hume Crawford had no idea how close he had been to the famed bandit and Tahoka intended to keep it that way. A thought entered the mind of the wounded warrior. If he could lead the bounty hunter across the border there might be far richer pickings for Crawford to concentrate upon.

Tahoka knew Zococa needed time. Time to fully recover. The wounded Apache was going to buy his friend as much time as he could, even if it meant sacrificing his own life.

He had managed the feat well until now.

The mute Apache fired again. His bullet hit the side wall of the cantina and forced Crawford to move even further back. Tahoka knew that if he rode from the stable right now, he would not reach the street before the bounty hunter. Even if he managed to cross the courtyard without Crawford shooting his horse out from under him, all the lethal bounty hunter would have to do was simply race through the cantina to the street and shoot him as he emerged from the alley.

He had to do something more cunning.

What would Zococa do? How would the man who had saved his life get the better of Crawford in this situation? Tahoka desperately tried to think of a plan: a course of action that would turn the tables on the gunman who had him trapped. No matter how hard he tried Tahoka could not think of anything.

He reloaded his rifle and then realized that he could no longer see Crawford near the doorway. As his bloody fingers forced the last bullet from his belt into the rifle's magazine he heard a noise that alarmed him, coming from the interior of the cantina.

To his horror he heard screaming. It was the hysterical screaming of a female being manhandled. Tahoka gripped his rifle and glared through the narrow gap between the wall and the door until his hooded eyes saw a young girl of about fourteen being forced out into the courtyard by Crawford.

The brutal bounty hunter had his left arm around her neck and held a gun to her temple with his right hand.

Crawford was using her as a shield, Tahoka grimly told himself. He was living up to his reputation.

'Ya best come out or I'll kill this sweet-looking gal, Injun,' Crawford shouted at the stable. 'I'm giving ya a minute to make up ya mind.'

The girl struggled but Crawford's powerful hands kept her between himself and the stable. He continued to force her forward. She continued to scream in fear and pain.

Tahoka knew he had to do something fast or the crazed bounty hunter would squeeze his trigger and blow her head apart. He knew that Crawford was not bluffing. Crawford never bluffed.

He just killed.

The Apache turned and walked to his horse. He slid his rifle into its saddle scabbard, lowered his head and stared at the ground. He saw the sand at his feet becoming red as his blood continued to drip from the hideous bullet hole in his chest.

There was no way he could allow a young female to be slain, he thought as he looked around the stable. He was about to give himself up when an idea entered his head. It was one that could have been concocted by Zococa himself.

Tahoka knew that he was a dead man unless he could create a distraction. What better distraction could there be than a fire?

Fire meant smoke. Smoke could blind even the keenest eyes from being able to see their target, he reasoned. Anything which could hamper Crawford's aim was worth trying. Tahoka looked around the stable. He had the makings of an inferno at his fingertips. There were two bales of hay in the corner of the stable and an oil lantern hanging on a nail directly above them.

Tahoka reached into his pants pocket and pulled out a handful of matches. He moved past his horse and dragged both the bales to the wide doorway. Tahoka then grabbed the lantern, removed its glass funnel and poured the oil over the dry hay. Then he slid half a dozen bullets from his gunbelt and dropped them on to one of the bales.

The Apache mounted his horse and hung low so that he was able to look beneath the animal's neck. He encouraged the black gelding towards the open doorway. He paused, struck one of the matches with his thumbnail, then dropped it on to the hay. Instantly flames leapt upward. The bone-dry rafters above his head caught alight. The fire spread across the wooden beams. Choking black smoke filled the small stable in seconds and poured out into the courtyard. He could see the confusion in the bounty hunter's face as he stared from behind his human shield at the blazing stable.

Tahoka remained hanging to the side of his terrified horse. Then, as the dense cloud of black smoke engulfed him, Tahoka reached back and whipped the rump of his horse as hard as he could. The horse did not hesitate. It charged through the flames and smoke that were billowing out into the yard.

A whirlpool of choking smoke and

burning embers masked the black horse as Tahoka hung next to its shoulder. It enveloped both horse and master as Crawford blasted his six-shooter blindly, trying to find a target. Then the bounty hunter saw the horse through the clouds of smoke. For a brief moment he thought that Tahoka must still be inside the stable.

Cocking his gun hammer again Crawford swung round and fired another shot into the flames. Then the terrified girl pulled away from her captor just as a rolling black cloud swept over them.

As Crawford managed to grab hold of her hair the bullets that the warrior had dropped into the hay bales exploded in venomous fury. Red-hot tapers of lethal lead cut through the smoke in every direction. Crawford ducked. At the very same moment Tahoka pulled himself up on top of his mount, whipped his reins and raced towards the gunman.

Fearlessly the Apache rode through the swirling smoke at the gunman and his hostage. Crawford suddenly heard the noise of the horse as it emerged through the swirling smoke. To his horror he saw the snorting animal charging towards him and the wailing young female.

The bounty hunter was about to fire when the young female sank her teeth into his wrist. Crawford yelped and released his grip on her. He went to strike her with his .45 but it was too late. Tahoka emerged from the smoke and drove his gelding straight at the bounty hunter. As Crawford raised his weapon Tahoka kicked it from the bounty hunter's hand. The Apache then reached down and took hold of the young female's arm. He swung her up behind him just as Crawford drew his other .45.

The Apache kicked his gelding's flanks and charged into Crawford. The horse knocked the bounty hunter off his feet, sending him crashing into the dust.

As the smoke filled the entire courtyard Tahoka steered his mount to the alley and thundered back to the street. On reaching the dry fountain the warrior stopped his horse and helped his passenger to disembark. Tahoka watched as the young girl fled into a side street, then he rode to where the grey stallion was tethered.

He pulled a knife from his belt, leaned over and cut the reins of Crawford's mount. Knowing that it would take the bounty hunter hours to find another bridle in Rio Cortez, Tahoka swung his horse round and thundered north.

Not until the black horse was galloping through the sun-baked streets did Tahoka feel the agonizing pain of the bullet in his chest.

Once again he was leaving an easy trail for the bounty hunter to follow. Tahoka aimed his black mount out of Rio Cortez and headed for the unmarked border. He knew that with each stride his mount was taking he was leading his deadly follower further and further away from Zococa.

The Apache warrior had whipped his long leathers across his horse's tail and ridden into Texas. He owed the Mexican bandit his life and was willing to sacrifice his own in order to repay that debt.

Tahoka had bought his friend a precious gift.

Time.

Most rational men knew when to quit but not those who were possessed by a festering evil that only dishing out death could ever satisfy. It was like a thirst that was impossible to quench. Hume Crawford staggered out of the cantina with his smoking guns gripped in his hands. Blood poured from a gash across his crazed features as he made his way to his horse. Then his fury erupted as his eyes caught sight of his severed reins.

The dust still hung in the dry, sun-baked street. The bounty hunter could still hear the echoing of the fleeing Apache's mount as Tahoka headed away from the sprawling town.

The snorting Crawford glanced all around him; then, up a narrow street, he saw the young girl whom Tahoka had rescued from his deadly grasp. She was huddled up beside a house door which refused to open.

The rage inside the lethal hunter of men could not be quelled as Crawford turned and walked towards her terrified form.

Her small clenched fists beat on the flaking paintwork of the door as she watched the man close the distance between them and heard the menacing jingle of his spurs.

'There ya are,' Crawford growled like a rabid dog with the scent of its prey in its flared nostrils. He holstered one of his guns and checked the one still in his grip. With each step he replaced the spent bullets with fresh ones from his gunbelt. By the time he had reached her his .45 was fully loaded again.

Crawford stopped. She was only a few inches away from his rancid body. The stench of his soiled, bloodstained clothing was sickening to a beautiful creature who had yet to lose her purity.

She pressed her back against the door and looked up into his fiery eyes. She wanted to scream but she could not utter a single sound.

He leaned even closer and pressed the barrel of his gun into her stomach.

'Ya bit me,' Crawford snarled, showing her the teeth marks on his wrist. 'Bit me so I lost sight of that Injun. It's your fault he escaped. I gotta punish ya for doing that. Savvy?'

Her tear-filled eyes looked up into his and she slowly nodded her head. She still could not speak. Terror had gripped her throat tighter than any hangman's noose could ever have done. She could feel his stinking body and his gun pressing against her and started to sob silently. Her naive mind began to fear what he intended to do to her as punishment for having sunk her teeth into him.

Crawford raised his free hand, traced a finger over her beautiful face, and pulled her mouth open. He was mocking her. He was daring her to repeat her action, but although young and innocent she was not a fool. He slid his filthy digit into her mouth as though wanting her to bite him again.

She did not want to die, though. She knew that there was only one way to survive against his overwhelming power, and that was to submit to any indignity he chose to dish out.

'Ya ain't so feisty now, are ya?' the bounty hunter mocked as he ran his hand down from her face on to her still developing body.

Her eyes screwed up as he gripped one of her breasts and rotated it perversely. She might have been young but she knew all too well what a certain type of man did when they got their hands on females unable to defend themselves.

Then suddenly there was a muffled sound as he squeezed the trigger of his .45. She felt the savage heat of the bullet as it tore through her. Within seconds she went limp but she did not fall until he stepped back from her.

Crawford watched as the young

female slid to the ground at his feet. A crimson scar marked her route down to the sand. Her once white blouse was blackened by the smoke from his gun. Then blood gushed from the hideous wound and spread across its thin fabric. He grunted, then spat on her.

The smoking barrel of his gun was covered in gore as he thrust it back into his holster.

'That'll teach ya. Nobody bites Hume Crawford and lives to tell the tale.' The bounty hunter swung round and started back towards his horse. The sound of his spurs rang out ominously to every living soul in the town.

The streets of Rio Cortez remained empty. No one would risk investigating until they were convinced that the lethal killing machine had departed once and for all.

4

A thousand shadows danced on either side of the narrow draw near the creek. The flames of the fire gave the temporary camp an almost devilish light which, added to the eerie illumination cast down by the large moon, was a cocktail that could play tricks even with the star riders' eyes. The flickering flames seemed to bring animation to every tree branch as well as the dense undergrowth that surrounded them. Red sparks rose up into the heavens as Marshal Hal Gunn piled more brushwood on to the already blazing campfire.

The wily marshal knew that only wild beasts were deterred by fire. Two-legged animals tended to be drawn to anywhere there was light. That was exactly what Gunn wanted. He wanted to draw to them the strange rider whom he and his deputy had spotted on the high rise.

Years of experience had taught Gunn that there were only two breeds of men who tracked star riders. Those who wanted to talk and those who wanted to kill.

Gunn was curious. He wanted to know which type their follower belonged to.

Most men would have chosen to spur hard to put as much distance as they could between themselves and the unknown horseman, but not Gunn.

He was cut from a different kind of cloth. He had never fled with his tail between his legs like so many other men tend to do when faced with possible danger. That had never been his way.

He always went forward where so many others ran backwards and that was why he had become a lawman, years earlier. They say that curiosity has killed many cats but cowardice has probably accounted for even more. Gunn never willingly offered his broad back as a target. He faced his demons.

Gunn rested the coffee pot in the flames and placed the blackened skillet next to it. He eyed his nervous deputy and grinned.

'We'll have us full bellies even if we don't lure that stranger down here, Toby,' Gunn said. He glanced to their mounts near the creek. 'Did ya secure their reins firmly? I don't want them breaking free when the shooting starts. This ain't no country to be on foot in.'

'I secured them real well. I even tied their legs together to stop them from hurting themselves,' Toby Jones replied with a sigh.

'That's fine, boy.'

Toby looked like a lamb that had been staked out as bait for a hungry mountain lion. He sat on his saddle close to the fire and looked hard at Gunn.

'I sure hope ya joshing with me, Marshal.'

'You and me both.' Gunn crouched down and looked into the troubled face of his young deputy. Toby folded his arms. He could not hide the fear which gripped his every sinew.

'I sure got me a real bad feeling about this.' Toby sighed again, then stood up and looked anxiously at the firelight as it played upon the trees and brush all around them. 'I'm starting to see things in every damn leaf on them trees.'

Gunn nodded. 'Ya know something? The most fearful thing in the whole world is what's inside a man's head, Toby. Every monster and demon ever created started off inside some man or woman's head.'

'That don't cut no mustard with me,' Toby said. 'I'm not figuring on any monsters getting me, but I sure reckon some critter with a gun might try his luck. This damn fire is so bright we ought to be drawing every damn outlaw for a hundred miles.'

'Quit beefing. Get the bacon out of the saddle-bags, son,' Gunn said. His eyes scanned the brush that fringed both sides of the gulch. 'And get that pork fat as well.'

Toby leaned over to the bag next to his saddle and opened one of its flaps. He pulled out the slab of bacon and the fat and tossed them to the marshal. 'I ain't hungry.'

The older lawman pulled a knife from his belt and unfolded its blade. He peeled the paper from the block of fat and dropped it into the centre of the skillet. It sounded like a rattler hissing as it rolled around the pan and melted.

'We're both gonna eat this grub, Toby,' Gunn said firmly. 'Eat our fill and drink every drop of our coffee. If we get killed I sure don't wanna get to heaven hungry.'

'So ya do admit we're in danger?'

'The moment a man pins a star to his shirt he's in danger, boy,' Gunn said. 'You know that. It's the price we pay for being star riders.'

The deputy leaned towards the flames, which leapt up towards the stars. 'I ain't got me no appetite. I'm troubled and no mistake.'

'Why?'

Toby raised his eyebrows. 'We're targets, Marshal. Ya made us targets. This fire is sure to bring that rider down from the ridge and I don't like the idea of him being able to pick us off from somewhere in the brush.'

'We've been targets since we first became lawmen, Toby.'

Toby rubbed his neck. 'This is different. That stranger can creep up on us and use us for target practice. I like to see who the hell is shooting at me. This could turn into a turkey shoot and we're the damn turkeys.'

'Stop fretting. He might not pick us off.' Gunn shrugged. He started to cut the bacon up and dropped the slices into the skillet. 'He might not be looking to kill us. He might be a drifter who happens to be lost and is looking for some friendship out here in the barren wastelands.'

'Horse feathers.'

Gunn smiled. 'Try and calm down. Smell the bacon. Don't it just make ya mouth water?'

'I ain't got no spittle to water with,' the deputy grumbled. 'I'm too scared to make no damn spittle.'

'He ain't meaning us no harm,' Gunn said. 'He could have shot us a long time back.'

Toby swallowed hard. 'I wish I was as sure about that as you are, Marshal.'

Gunn rubbed his greasy gloved hands down his pants legs and dropped on to one knee. 'Have a little faith, boy.'

'Hell. If that varmint sneaks up on us and starts shooting from out there in the brush, we don't stand a chance.' The deputy gave out a long sigh. 'We're sitting ducks by this fire and ya know it.'

'First we was turkeys and now we're ducks,' Gunn observed. He poked the bacon with his knife and gave the skillet a shake. The bacon began to sizzle and spit. 'I always try to look on the bright side. Reckon you ought to try and do the same.'

Toby stood up and rested his hand on his holstered gun grip. His eyes searched the trees and bushes as the flickering light of their campfire danced upon the branches. Then the young star rider screwed up his eyes and looked to the moonlit ridge far above them. He turned and looked down at the older man.

'He's gone. He ain't up there no more, Marshal,' Toby gasped and his finger poked at the air frantically. 'Look. The critter must have headed on down here just like I said he would.'

'I don't have to look, Toby,' Gunn said and continued to concentrate on the frying bacon.

The deputy frowned. He was utterly confused by Gunn's imperturbability. 'How come ya don't have to look up there for ya to know that he ain't up on that rim any more?'

'That's simple. I saw him start down from there as soon as I lit this fire,' Gunn replied. He continued to work on their supper.

Toby gasped. 'And ya didn't tell me?'

'Nope.'

The younger man leaned over the

marshal. 'He could be anywhere and ya just kneeling there frying bacon. We ain't got a clue where that rider is.'

Gunn glanced up. 'I know where his horse is.'

'What?'

The marshal pulled the skillet off the fire and rested it on the sand. He stood up to his full height and looked beyond his deputy's shoulder with narrowed eyes. 'Turn round, Toby.'

Toby Jones spun on his heels and stared at the black mount as it walked out from the brush. There was no rider upon its saddle. The animal strolled slowly towards the creek where their own mounts were tethered. Both lawmen watched the animal as it reached the water, lowered its head and began drinking.

'I . . . I don't get it,' Toby stammered.

'Kinda confusing, ain't it?' Gunn said.

'What's going on, Marshal?'

Gunn inhaled and nodded knowingly. He strode from the campfire to the drinking saddle horse and studied the animal. He looked at his deputy at his shoulder. 'I recognize this horse, Toby. Don't you?'

Toby looked at the horse carefully and scratched his neck. 'What? Sure it's a fair bet that it's been ridden long and hard, but how can ya say that ya recognize it? It's only a dumb horse.'

'Look.' Gunn pointed at the saddle. There was a familiar mark carved in its leather cantle. It was one which the older lawmen recognized. It was a strange symbol that he had seen on only two saddles before, but he had good reason to remember it. Yet even though he knew that he had seen the mark on the saddles of Zococa and his mute Apache friend Tahoka, Gunn realized that that did not mean the mysterious rider they had spotted just after sundown was either of them. Horses were often stolen on both sides of the long, unmarked border. Even though Gunn was certain that the black horse belonged to the huge Apache, it did not mean that Tahoka had been the rider whom they had seen.

86

'I recall that mark, Marshal,' Toby said. 'It's the one Zococa and his pal had carved on their saddles, ain't it?'

'Yep,' Gunn replied.

Toby nodded. 'Damn it all. This is the horse big old Tahoka rode.'

Suddenly Gunn felt uneasy. The hair on the nape of his neck tingled beneath his bandanna. A cold shiver raced the length of his spine. He turned slowly, then his eyes widened as they focused upon a shadowy figure silently moving close to the edge of the dense brush to their right.

Both the star riders were aware that the owner of the lathered-up horse that had just entered their temporary camp had them both in his gun sights. The flickering light of the campfire's flames traced along the metal barrel of the Winchester, which was held at hip level and aimed right at them by a figure shrouded in blackness.

'Look, Marshal,' Toby croaked as he pointed at the deadly rifle. 'Someone's got a carbine aimed at us.'

'I see it, son,' Gunn replied. He walked away from the horses and stood between the rifle and his young friend.

'What we gonna do?'

'Don't move a muscle, Toby,' Gunn ordered his deputy, in a tone that demanded obedience. 'Whatever ya do don't go for ya gun. I reckon it'd be a real bad mistake.'

* * *

At almost the same moment, fifteen miles south, Hume Crawford crossed the unmarked boundary between Texas and Mexico and jerked back on his reins. His horse needed food and water but the vicious bounty hunter refused to delay his pursuit of the fleeing Tahoka. Every part of him had grown to believe that, like a wounded animal, the Apache was seeking his friend Zococa and a place to die. Crawford had not rested since he had ridden from Rio Cortez. He knew that he was getting closer with every stride his tall grey stallion took.

With the light of the moon behind him he leaned from his saddle and stared at the sand in front of his horse's hoofs. He could clearly make out the tracks of unshod hoofs left by the warrior's mount. Crawford could also see the droplets of blood left by the man he pursued.

Crawford straightened up on his horse. He was about to continue following the well-defined trail when something half a mile away from him drew his evil attention.

The horseman dragged his new reins hard around and stared through the eerie moonlight. For a moment he thought that he had caught a fleeting glimpse of a wild animal. He was about to return his attention to the decoy tracks left by Tahoka when he noticed a faint, flickering light. A group of trees between the light and the rider obscured Crawford's view but it did not stop the curious horseman from ramming his spurs into his grey and heading towards it.

After he had travelled no more than

200 yards the bounty hunter noticed that the unshod tracks were suddenly in front of him.

Tahoka had also ridden this way, Crawford told himself.

The closer he got to the trees the clearer the light became. There was a wooden cabin set on a slight rise. As the horseman got closer he could see an open window and an oil lamp set just inside the cabin.

Crawford kept looking from the ground to the cabin. The unshod tracks led straight to the wooden structure. Then he heard the sound of a man's voice.

The lethal horseman stopped his mount near the trees and dismounted quickly. He tied his reins to one of the numerous leafless branches and proceeded forward until he was standing by the window.

A bearded old man was pottering around inside the interior of the small cabin. Like most people who live alone, he spoke to himself continuously.

Crawford drew one of his guns from

its holster and walked round to the closed door. He raised a boot and kicked at the door with all his might.

As it was ripped from its rusted hinges the bounty hunter strode inside and stared at the stunned occupant. The man was shaking as he returned Crawford's gaze.

'Tahoka's been here,' Crawford declared. He moved to the old man and pushed his gun into the man's neck. 'Which way did he head?'

The bearded man blinked hard. 'Ya mean the Injun?'

'Right first time, old-timer.' Crawford snorted. 'Which way did he head after he left here?'

'North.' The bearded old man gestured with a thin arm.

'Where up north?'

The old man looked totally bemused. 'There's only one place between here and El Diablo. Hal Gunn's cattle spread.'

'Marshal Gunn?' Crawford queried.

The old man nodded. 'Yep. That's the varmint. Do ya know him?'

'We've locked horns before.' Crawford turned and walked back to the doorway. As he reached what was left of the broken door he paused and looked at the squinting figure. 'By the way, how old are ya, old-timer?'

The old man looked puzzled. 'Reckon I must be close to seventy. Why'd ya ask?'

Crawford fanned his gun hammer. His deadly accurate shot hit the old man in his temple. The bounty hunter watched as the bearded man flew backwards and crashed into the far wall before crumpling into a heap on the floor.

'I reckon you've lived long enough.'

Crawford made his way back to his grey stallion. As he tugged his reins free and stepped into his stirrup he thought about the words of the old man he had just slaughtered. Tahoka had headed north and the only place between El Diablo and this desolate place was Hal Gunn's ranch.

'That has to be where Zococa is hiding.'

Crawford spurred.

5

Firelight of an unearthly scarlet hue filled the camp of the star riders. The flames pulsated upward into the sky above the lawmen. But no matter how bright the illumination of the campfire grew as it consumed the dry brushwood that Gunn had stacked high over the white-hot centre of the contained inferno, it did not reach the shadowy rifleman. Whoever he was, he was hidden from view by the trees and the entangled bushes.

Gunn stepped forward and squinted hard.

Was this the mute Indian brave who was aiming his rifle at them? The question raced like quicksilver through Gunn's mind.

Tahoka was a mystery to them. He had been the shadow of the famous Zococa and had done everything the

Mexican bandit had instructed him to do. He was fearless, just like his more flamboyant companion. Neither of the lawmen could understand why he would be holding a rifle on them. There were many unanswered questions in the minds of both Gunn and Toby.

Maybe he did not recognize them.

If it was Tahoka, why was he alone?

Had the Comancheros against whom they had all battled eighteen months before managed to do what so many others had failed to achieve?

Had their bullets killed the colourful bandit who had boasted that he was a legend and that legends never died? Had Zococa's brutal wounds made him unable to keep his promise to Gunn's young daughter?

Was he dead?

Then both of the lawmen started to dwell upon their other theory as they stared across the sand at the gleaming rifle barrel. What if someone had stolen Tahoka's mount? Both the star riders knew that if this was actually a vengeful gunman set on getting even for some unknown reason, they were doomed.

There was no cover to protect them if the rifle started spewing lead at them.

'I'm starting to figure that it ain't Tahoka, Marshal,' Toby said with a gulp.

Gunn bit his lip. 'That's gotta be Tahoka, Toby. It's just gotta be him.'

'We're dead men, Marshal,' Toby blurted out and his stare remained on the deadly rifle barrel that poked out from the bushes. 'I knew it was a mistake to stop here. We should have kept on riding. We'd be halfway home by now.'

'We ain't dead yet, son,' Gunn said.

'As good as, Marshal,' Toby argued. 'That can't be Tahoka who's got the drop on us. He'd not pull a rifle on us.'

'He did the first time we met, as I recall,' Gunn remembered. 'Maybe he don't recognize us. It's dark and he's a wanted bandit. Maybe he's just being cautious.'

'Why's he on his lonesome?' Toby whispered. 'Why ain't Zococa with him?'

Gunn glanced at his younger pal. 'Don't ya recall the condition of Zococa the last time we seen him? He was riddled with lead, boy. I don't think even he could have survived no matter how he promised little Polly.'

'What if that's just some horse thief yonder?' Toby swallowed hard. 'If he gets himself a glimpse of our stars he might just start squeezing that rifle trigger, Marshal.'

'I'd agree, but by my figuring, even a horse thief would have started shooting by now.' Gunn rubbed his gloved thumb across his lips. 'Stealing horses is a hanging offence. That critter has to be Tahoka.'

'Why don't he show himself, then?' Toby was anxious.

'There's only one way to find out,' Gunn said firmly.

'Ya ain't thinking of going over there, are ya?'

Gunn did not reply. As had always been his habit he started to walk towards the rifle, which was still aimed in their direction. Once again he had decided to face his fears and not run away from them.

With each stride Gunn saw the shadowy image grow larger but no clearer. With every step he felt his heart quicken inside his chest. He knew that he might be wrong and that he could be heading towards his own executioner. Gunn paced slowly but surely towards the trees. There was no turning back. He had to discover the truth.

Gunn was positive that it had to be Tahoka. The light of the campfire glinted on the rifle barrel as it slowly tracked the marshal. Anyone else would have fired by now, Gunn told himself.

Then, as he got within twenty feet of the rifle, another thought flashed through Gunn's mind. What if Toby was right after all? What if Tahoka's horse had been stolen by a merciless killer?

The sound of the rifle being cocked filled the clearing.

Gunn stopped in his tracks. 'Damn. I wonder why he up and primed that carbine?'

There was a long, nervous silence. The marshal looked back at his deputy. Toby was frozen like a statue beside the three horses near the creek. The young deputy did not know what to do for the best. Any sudden movement from either of the star riders might be seen as a provocation. It might be punished by rifle bullets.

Gunn licked his dry lips and inhaled deeply. He was not just sucking in air but sucking in every scrap of courage he could muster. He looked straight ahead at the shadowy figure set just back from the trees.

'Is that you, Tahoka?' Gunn called out.

There was another seemingly endless pause. The rifle remained aimed at the marshal. The figure did not move a muscle. Whoever he was he was hidden from view by the dense undergrowth. Not even the flickering light of the campfire could penetrate it and find him.

The marshal took one step. 'Look at me, Tahoka. Remember me? I'm Hal Gunn and that's young Toby. Don't ya recall? We're ya pals.'

Toby took a few steps and paused. 'Is it Tahoka?'

The marshal urgently raised a hand to his deputy. 'Stay there, son.'

The younger star rider stopped. He clenched both his fists at his sides. Every sinew in his body wanted to do something to help the man he had grown to think of as a father. Yet there was nothing he could do. Toby knew he was helpless to do anything without endangering Gunn.

'Is it him?' Toby again called out. Again Gunn did not respond to the question. The older of the star riders screwed up his eyes and peered into the dense undergrowth, but still he was unable to make out the rifleman. All he could see was a looming dark shape and the shining rifle, which was still trained upon him.

'Damn it all,' Gunn snapped at the rifle. 'Is that you, Tahoka? If it is, show yourself. We got grub yonder. Are ya hungry?'

The rifle was jutting out from the bushes. Not even the hands of its owner could be seen from the clearing. Gunn knew that if it was Tahoka, the Apache would be unable to reply but he should respond somehow. Gunn wished he had the ability to talk with his hands like the flamboyant Zococa. Or at least be able to read the gestures he had seen the huge Apache use when speaking to the Mexican bandit. How did you communicate with someone who had had his tongue savagely cut from his mouth and could only speak with his hands and fingers?

The question burned like a branding-iron into the star rider as he ignored his own terror and defiantly took another tentative step forward.

The young deputy was terrified that any moment a deadly flash of gun-smoke would kill Gunn.

'Come on back, Marshal,' Toby pleaded as he stood helplessly beside the three drinking horses. 'Whoever that is he's just toying with ya. He's gonna blow ya apart.'

Marshal Gunn glanced over his shoulder and shouted, 'Hush up, boy. I'm feared enough without ya telling me what this critter might do. Don't ya think I ain't figured that out already?'

Suddenly there was movement in the undergrowth. The sound of twigs snapping underfoot filled the air. The older lawman gave out a long, troubled sigh. He swallowed hard and for the first time since he had stopped to make camp, Gunn began to doubt his own wisdom. Yet even as beads of sweat ran down from his hatband and stung his eyes Gunn defied his own fear and took another step forward.

To his surprise and relief the rifle did not fire. Gunn stopped again and looked down at his feet. His mind was racing. If it was the mute Apache he wondered what he was doing here. Gunn's memory went back to the last time he had seen the massive Indian. Tahoka had been cradling the severely wounded Mexican bandit Zococa in his huge arms astride the bandit's pinto stallion.

Zococa was as close to death as any man could get but had hidden his horrific wounds from the eyes of Gunn's daughter with his sombrero. For some unknown reason the famed bandit had risked his life to save Virginia and little Polly. It had cost him dear.

Gunn looked back up at the shadows. 'Where's Zococa, my friend? Is he still alive?'

Suddenly the rifle was lowered and the massive Apache stepped out into the moonlight. The light from the flames of the campfire illuminated Tahoka. What it displayed was not what Gunn had expected.

Gunn again swallowed hard. The warrior, who seemed to be even larger than the lawman remembered him to be, was covered in blood.

For a moment Tahoka did nothing but stare with his hooded eyes at the star rider. Gunn could not conceal his dismay at the sight of the blood-covered buckskin shirt front. Blood was glistening in the eerie light as it pumped from the bullet hole just below the Apache's left collarbone.

'Ya wounded!' Gunn exclaimed as he stepped towards the big man.

Tahoka looked at him, gave a slight nod of his head, then crashed to the ground like a felled tree. The star rider dropped on to his knees beside the Indian. Within seconds the sand started to darken as blood spread from the hideous bullet wound. Gunn tried to turn the huge figure over but it was impossible. Tahoka was far too heavy.

Gunn looked to his deputy. 'Get over here, Toby.'

Toby ran across the sand to where the marshal was kneeling next to the motionless Apache.

'Help me turn him over, son,' Gunn ordered.

Both of the star riders summoned every ounce of their strength and managed to turn Tahoka over on to his back. There was no sign of life in the sand-covered face of the unconscious warrior.

'Is he dead, Marshal?' Toby asked. He tried to wipe the debris from the noble features of the Apache. 'Is he?'

'I sure hope not.' Gunn frantically tore the buckskin shirt open. Its blood-soaked leather laces parted easily. The exposed chest was like a barrel. Yet it did not move. There was no sign of breathing. There was only an ocean of blood, which covered the expanse of Tahoka's torso. More of the crimson gore pumped out from the savage bullet hole with every passing second.

'Why'd ya figure he suddenly showed himself?' Toby asked the marshal. 'Ya was talking to him for the longest while and he stayed hidden. What did ya say that drew him out?'

'I asked him about Zococa,' Gunn answered. 'I asked him if Zococa was still alive.'

'It must have been him hearing Zococa's name that made him realize who ya was, Marshal,' Toby said. 'I wonder where Zococa is? I wonder if he is still alive? That might be why Tahoka is alone.'

'If Tahoka dies we'll never find out, Toby boy.' Gunn pressed his hand down on the chest of the Apache warrior. 'I can feel his heart beating, Toby. It's beating like a war drum.'

'It's gonna stop beating real soon if he keeps bleeding like this, though, Marshal,' the deputy said. 'It's a good thing he's as big as he is. He must have a whole lot more blood than most normal-sized folks.'

'Ya right.' Gunn pressed down on the wound in an attempt to stop the bleeding. 'Go put our knives in the fire. We got to heat them both up.'

'Are ya gonna cut the bullet out, Marshal?' Toby asked. He raced towards the fire.

'I'm gonna try, Toby boy,' Gunn answered. 'I'm gonna surely try.'

6

For nearly eighteen months the famed Mexican bandit had spent more time asleep than awake as he fought his most important battle. His injuries had been so severe and life-threatening that for most of that time it had seemed that he might never fully regain consciousness. Yet Luis Santiago Rodrigo Vallencio was no ordinary man and had defied death for most of his adult life. He had become better known as the legendary Zococa and had miraculously proved his boast that legends can never die.

But even legends need a helping hand when they have been riddled with bullets. The church in San Remo had served the people of the region for nearly a hundred years, but its handful of priests had never been called upon to save the life of someone who seemed to be almost dead until his large Apache companion had arrived with his blood-stained body cradled in his powerful arms.

This had been a challenge greater than any the priests could have imagined they would ever be called upon to meet.

In a land where there were no doctors the priests managed to deliver the basics of crude medical assistance for those who required it. They had the knowledge to set broken bones and in their herb gardens they grew the ingredients for a dozen medicines, but Tahoka had set them a far greater challenge than merely setting a broken leg. For the first time the priests would have to attempt to do what few real doctors had ever successfully managed. They had to remove half a dozen bullets from the famed Zococa's body.

It would have proved to be a daunting task even for a qualified surgeon but to the priests it had seemed to be utterly impossible. Yet they had faith that their sharpest of knives would be guided. Their faith was justified.

Somehow their patient had survived. Somehow their combined prayers and unyielding belief had achieved what many considered to be unachievable.

Yet even though their patient had not died as they had feverishly worked to save his life, Zococa had remained in a coma for over a year.

Then, slowly, the young bandit managed to fight his way out of his deep sleep and regain consciousness. The church at San Remo had a library of books that told of miracles, but now the holy men had witnessed one for themselves. Their most fervent prayers had been answered.

Day after day Zococa gained strength. Yet it had taken another two long months after he had awoken before he was able to set his feet on the ground and start the tedious task of strengthening his legs until they were strong enough to support his weight.

For the bandit who had always been so flamboyant and self-assured it had proved to be a humbling time. Zococa had never been a man who liked to owe anything to others, but he knew that he now owed debts that he would never be able to repay, no matter how long he lived.

He owed the priests for their skill, faith and selfless consideration for a virtual stranger. They had all played a part in his survival.

He also owed Tahoka for bringing him to the church.

The mute warrior had no way of knowing it but he had helped the priests achieve something that none of them had ever considered possible.

He had allowed them to participate in a miracle.

★   ★   ★

For the previous month Zococa had been able to walk around his room. At one time it had been a cell where novices of the church slept. At first the bandit had used sticks to enable him to remain upright and walk. Then, as the muscles of his legs gradually regained their strength Zococa found he no longer needed sticks. He could walk unaided, but had little stamina. That would also return in time.

What the famed bandit did not know was that his time in the sanctuary of the church was about to run out. There was no time left to rekindle his once untold stamina. Something had awoken him from a nightmarish dream and chilled him to his very soul.

Beads of sweat trailed down his handsome face and dripped on to the scars of his now healed chest. He swallowed hard and gazed around the room. The first rays of a new day spread over him as he threw the blankets aside and lowered his feet on to the cold floor.

The nightmare had seemed so real.

Zococa was still shaking as he tried to compose himself and gather his thoughts together.

'Tahoka,' he heard himself mutter as the terrifying memory of the obscure dream returned to haunt him. 'Tahoka is in trouble.'

His eyes flashed around the room for his faithful companion. The cot across the room was still empty and unused as it had been for several weeks. He rose to his feet, walked to the cot and stared down upon it. The confusing dream had made him forget that he had not seen his friend for weeks, but now a dread had crept into Zococa.

He feared for his friend's safety.

Every sinew in his lean body ached as he rested a hand on the wall. What had frightened him so much? Zococa asked himself. Why had he seen Tahoka in his nightmare?

Even though he had not seen the Apache brave for weeks he had not thought anything of it. Tahoka was a free spirit who often hunted alone without the hindrance of Zococa.

'What is wrong, my son?' the reassuring voice of Father Pablo asked the obviously disturbed bandit as he entered with a tray of food. 'You look as though you have seen a ghost.'

Zococa's eyes darted to the priest. 'I

had a nightmare, Father. A nightmare and Tahoka was in it. He was in trouble and in pain.'

Father Pablo placed the tray down on a small table set between the two cots. 'You are just frightened that something has happened to your friend, my son.'

'It was so real,' Zococa said, rubbing his sweat-soaked neck with the palm of his hand. 'It was as if my little elephant was calling out to me to help him. I know this is loco, for my friend cannot talk, but I swear by all that is holy that Tahoka was calling to me.'

'A dream,' Father Pablo said. 'You are still weak and you can expect nightmares until you regain your strength. Eat the food I have brought for you.'

'There is no time to eat, Father,' Zococa said firmly. He straightened up and moved to the small window. He looked down on to the courtyard. 'I must go to Tahoka.'

The priest moved to the side of the troubled bandit and placed a hand on his shoulder. 'You cannot leave now. You are still too weak. How can you help Tahoka when you have barely learned how to walk for more than a few hours without requiring rest?'

Zococa shook his head. 'Tahoka needs me, Father.'

'I tell you that it was just a bad dream, my son,' Father Pablo explained. 'Think about it. Tahoka could return when you are out there looking for him.'

The bandit walked to his clothes. He lifted his shirt and began to dress. 'I have had many dreams in my life. I have never had one like that one, Father. Tahoka was calling out to me and I am the only one who can understand him. He is hurt or even worse. I must find him. I owe him. I must go.'

The priest had never seen the bandit so alarmed before.

'Perhaps you had a vision,' he suggested. 'I have heard that sometimes people have visions that no one can explain, my young friend.'

'Do you think I am loco, Father?'

Zococa asked. He pulled on his pants and then sat down to put on his boots.

Father Pablo looked hard at the young man. 'There was a time when I thought I would never see you open your eyes. I thought you would remain asleep until you joined the angels. No, Zococa. I do not think you are loco.'

Zococa paused. 'Angels. Why do I remember angels?'

The priest watched as Zococa rose to his feet with a confused expression on his handsome face. 'It is just a saying, my son.'

'No. It is more than that,' Zococa said. 'I remember angels in my dream. Talk of angels.'

Father Pablo was now the one who was confused. 'I do not understand any of this, my son. This is a church and there are many statues of angels. You have seen them all. Maybe you just dreamt of them.'

Zococa looked at the elderly priest. 'No. I saw a golden-haired angel, Father. She was with Tahoka.'

Father Pablo gripped the golden cross hanging from his neck and raised it to his lips. He kissed it, then lowered it again.

'Are you determined to leave, my son?'

'*Sí*, Father.' Zococa picked up his gunbelt, looped it around his waist and secured its silver buckle. 'Can you get my horse readied?'

The priest nodded. 'I pray you will find your friend and the golden-haired angel.'

The handsome bandit smiled, then suddenly recalled the face of the angel he had seen in his dreams. He snapped his fingers.

'The little angel is the daughter of a very fine lawman, Father. I promised her I would not die and would return to see her one day.'

'Why would she be in your dream, my son?'

The famed bandit nodded. 'Maybe Tahoka is with her and her mother and father. Maybe my little elephant is hurt and with them. Could that be it?'

'I would not like to argue with a man who makes promises to angels, my son.' Father Pablo patted the arm of the bandit and turned to leave the room. 'I shall have your horse readied. Now eat your food.'

Zococa picked up his sombrero and looked at it. Even though it had been washed and dried it still showed the bloodstains it had picked up when its owner had shielded his horrific wounds from the innocent eyes of the little child.

The famed bandit placed the hat on and tightened its drawstring under his chin. His left hand rested on his silver pistol. He knew that San Remo was far closer to Marshal Gunn's cattle ranch across the border than it was to any of the neighbouring Mexican settlements. He knew every short cut in Texas and had used them all to elude capture by eager lawmen.

The young man ran his hands down his black clothing and was impressed by how well it had been repaired. The priests had employed San Remo's most skilled seamstresses to hide the bullet holes in the shirt and jacket. It was impossible to see the damage.

He was tired, though. Even the simple task of dressing had drained his once abundant strength. Zococa walked to the window and looked down into the courtyard.

A smile came to his handsome features as he saw two of the holy men lead his magnificent pinto stallion from the stable towards the church. He turned and inhaled deeply. The haunting dream returned to his troubled mind.

He then vowed firmly: 'I shall return to you, little Polly. Zococa never breaks a promise to a golden-haired angel. I shall find you and my little elephant.'

The bandit strode from the room.

7

There were savage scars across the centre of the cattle ranch that Hal Gunn had rebuilt after it had been razed to the ground by the ruthless Comancheros. The new buildings sat close to where blackened ground and two well-tended graves bore witness to what had occurred here only a year and a half earlier. This was now a scene of tranquillity, yet there was never a moment when any of those on the ranch ever truly relaxed any more. The memory of the brutal attack and slayings could not be extinguished from the minds of any of them. They were like the smouldering flames of a fire that refused ever to die down.

There was hope for a better future but it was built upon the foundations of a cruel past.

Ever since the unwarranted attack

and killings Hal Gunn had never allowed his wife and daughter to be alone on the remote cattle spread. He had hired two trusted cowboys not only to look after his growing herd but to guard his most precious possessions. His beautiful wife and daughter had to be protected whilst he was away fulfilling his duties as a border marshal.

The ranch and bunkhouse had been constructed far closer together than their original counterparts. Gunn knew that his two cowboys had to be able to get to the main house as quickly as possible, just in case history repeated itself. In this hostile land that often happened.

There were no more Comancheros like the ones he and Zococa had tackled, but there were always drifters. Most were harmless but some were cut from the same savage cloth as those who had invaded his ranch. Nothing could ever be taken for granted along the border.

Death was the only certainty the

living could actually count upon. It could come and strike its victims down at any time it chose. Fevers took the young and the old, and bullets never showed any discrimination.

Gunn knew he dared not risk the lives of what was left of his family. That was why he had decided to retire as a lawman so that he would never again have to spend even one more night away from Virginia or little Polly.

The handsome woman with long, flowing blonde hair walked from the ranch house. Her equally beautiful daughter was at her heels as always. Little Polly had grown far closer to her mother since they had returned to the ranch. She had become her mother's shadow.

This was a place that held memories; and some of them were far more frightening than a small child could be expected to cope with. Polly walked barefoot behind her mother and did what all little girls do: she copied her every action and gesture. If fate was kind she would one day have a daughter of her own who learned from her.

Virginia held her apron out in front of her. It was filled with chicken feed. She had forced herself to ignore her fears when her man was away from home. Every day was filled with well-practised rituals, designed to allow her to avoid dwelling upon those fears. But each night, when she had seen her daughter fall asleep, Virginia was alone in her matrimonial bed.

That was another reason why Gunn had resolved to become a full-time rancher. He had grown weary of being away from those he loved. They were the only people he really wanted to protect.

Virginia scattered the grain across the yard and watched as their numerous hens appeared from every direction and started pecking. No matter how many times she repeated this ritual it always made her small daughter giggle. The sun was hotter than usual and the sky showed no sign of it raining any time soon. Yet for some reason Virginia felt a cold chill race up her spine beneath her well-laundered dress. She stopped and stared around the land that fringed the cattle ranch.

Then she looked up to the ridge and her eyes narrowed.

She remembered the deadly riders who had gathered there and then attacked them. Her heart was racing but she did not know why. It was a beautiful day but something inside her felt uneasy. It was as though her stomach was knotted.

'What's wrong, Mommy?' Polly asked. Her little hand tugged on her mother's apron.

Virginia looked down at her child. Polly's face was no longer showing amusement. Now it only showed concern.

Virginia stroked her daughter's yellow hair and forced a smile. 'Nothing's wrong, Polly.'

'Promise?'

Hal Gunn's wife nodded. 'I promise.'

They both turned and walked back towards the ranch house. As they went Virginia waved a hand to one of the ranch hands who was just walking from the half-built barn. Billy Vale came running towards them.

'What's wrong, Ginny?' he asked.

'I don't know.' She ushered her daughter into the house and ran a hand over her graceful neck. 'I got me a feeling that something might be wrong, Billy.'

Billy knew that the sensible woman never cried wolf: she had learned the hard way to recognize when trouble was brewing. 'Ya want me and Rex to get our guns?'

She smiled and nodded. 'I think it might be wise. It's too quiet out there.'

The cowboy touched the brim of his hat. 'We'll keep our eyes open. Don't go fretting none. We'll not let anyone cause any trouble.'

Virginia smiled again. 'Thanks, Billy.'

When they reached the top of the steps in front of the open door of their home Polly asked, 'What's wrong, Mommy? Why was ya talking to Billy for?'

Virginia grabbed her daughter's pigtails. 'There's nothing wrong, Polly.

Let's make cookies.'

'Cookies? Is Pa due back?' There was excitement in the child's voice as they entered the house. 'Is he? Is he?'

'He sure is. Any time now.' Virginia closed the door and secretly slid the bolt across. She followed the small child into the kitchen and tried to keep smiling, even though she still had a sickening feeling deep inside her. 'I figure he'll be back even faster when he smells our cookies.'

'Why'd ya bolt the door?'

'We don't want the house full of flies when we're making cookies, do we?'

Polly accepted the answer.

Virginia placed a large mixing bowl on top of the sturdy table as Polly clambered up on to a chair and rested her elbows on the table's well-scrubbed surface.

'What do dreams mean, Mommy?'

Virginia glanced at her daughter. 'What do you mean?'

'I had me the nicest dream last night,' Polly revealed.

'What was your nice dream about?' Virginia asked. 'Let me guess. Was it about your Pa getting home?'

Polly shook her head. 'No. It was about Zococa.'

The woman paused. 'You still remember him?'

'Of course I do. He was so nice.' Polly sighed. 'He promised he'd come to see me.'

'That was a long time ago, Polly honey.'

'No it wasn't, Mommy. It was last night in my dream,' Polly corrected.

Virginia placed a bowl full of eggs on the table and looked at her daughter curiously. She pushed a few long strands of her blonde hair behind her ear and smiled. 'He might not be able to come here to see you, sweetheart. He was hurt really bad. Remember?'

'I'm not a baby.' Polly frowned. 'Of course I remember.'

Virginia continued to busy herself around the kitchen. She dropped a log down into the belly of the cooking range and replaced the large, blackened iron plate. 'The stove will be hot enough by the time we've mixed up the eggs,' she said.

'It'll be nice to see Zococa again,' Polly went on. 'I'm glad he's coming to see us.'

'Zococa was very ill,' Virginia reminded her. 'Sometimes when folks are really ill they can't get better.'

'He'll come to see me,' Polly insisted. 'You wait and see.'

Virginia Gunn nodded. 'I hope he does.'

Polly gave a huge smile. 'He thought I was an angel, Mommy. He was very funny. He said I was an angel. Remember?'

'Of course I remember, Polly.' Virginia grinned. 'I'm not a child.'

Polly looked at the ceiling. 'What's an angel?'

Virginia found a sack of flour and set it down next to the eggs. 'I'm not sure, but I think it must be someone who is very, very beautiful like you.'

Polly thought about the answer, then nodded. 'I think you're right, Mommy.'

8

A million nightmares paraded through the mind of the unconscious Tahoka as the two star riders propped him up against one of their saddles and tried to awaken him. Hal Gunn had managed to cut the bullet lead from the giant warrior's chest and had cauterized the wound with the red-hot blade of his knife more than half a day earlier, but for some reason Tahoka had not awoken.

'Why don't he wake up, Marshal?' Toby asked.

'I don't know, Toby,' Gunn admitted. 'But we can't leave him here like this. There's way too many pumas and wolves around. I reckon they'd sure have themselves a feast if they found a meal this big.'

'And there ain't no way we can get him up on his horse.' Toby sighed as he poured himself a cup of coffee and sipped at it. 'Reckon we're stuck here until he either dies or he opens his damn eyes.'

Hal Gunn was about to agree, then he had an idea. 'We need a wagon and we need a couple of men to help us load this old Apache on its flatbed, Toby boy.'

The deputy lowered the steaming tin cup from his lips and smiled. 'And you just happen to have a wagon and a couple of ranch hands at ya ranch, Marshal.'

The older star rider winked. 'Why don't ya saddle that nag of yours, head off to the ranch and round up them things, boy?'

Toby got to his feet and downed the remnants of his beverage. 'I reckon I'll do just that, Marshal. It's gotta be a lot better than hanging around here getting sun-baked.'

Gunn got to his feet and looked at the large Apache. He was troubled that even though he had managed to cut the lead out of Tahoka and stem the bleeding it might all have been in vain. The warrior had lost a lot of blood even for a man his size. Had Tahoka lost too much blood?

The question taunted the star rider.

The young deputy tightened his cinch strap, threw himself aboard his mount, then steadied the animal as the long-legged marshal walked towards him. There was concern in Gunn's weathered face.

Since the Comancheros had attacked his ranch a year and a half earlier and killed his son and Virginia's father, he had never allowed his wife and daughter to be alone. He had hired two trustworthy ranch hands to protect them when he was away fulfilling his duties as a star rider.

A chill raced up his spine as Toby stopped his horse close to him. He gripped the bridle and looked up hard into the face of his junior.

'On second thoughts, do ya reckon that we need both Billy and Rex to help us get this Apache up on the flatbed of the wagon, boy?' Gunn looked anxiously into the younger man's face.

Toby frowned. 'I sure do. What's eating ya, Marshal?'

Gunn did not respond to the question. He shrugged. 'Ya right. I'm just being a tad cautious, I guess.'

The deputy had grown to know his mentor far better than Gunn would ever realize. He nodded. 'Come to think on it I reckon Billy got enough muscle on his lonesome to help you and me haul Tahoka up on the back of the flatbed. Hell, Rex can stay back and look after Ginny and Polly. He's a skinny critter even when he's got himself a full belly. He'd be no help at all.'

The marshal released the bridle and beamed a smile up at Toby. 'I think ya right, Toby. Best if ya leave Rex to look after the womenfolk.'

'I'll be back as fast I can, Marshal.' Toby swung his mount full circle and spurred. Gunn watched the horse cross the creek and then disappear into the heat haze. The star rider knew that his young friend had understood his unspoken words, showing him that he had learned a lot more than either of them had imagined.

The marshal gave a long sigh, then turned round and headed back towards the massive Tahoka. He had not taken three steps when he saw something move through the brush a couple of hundred yards away. It was a horseman with the sun at his back. The rider then stopped. Gunn squinted hard in the direction of the rider. He could not make out who it was. All he could tell was that the new arrival was wearing a wide-brimmed sombrero.

Faster than he had ever drawn his .45 before, Gunn hauled the Colt from its holster in one swift action and trained it upon the unexpected visitor. His thumb pulled back on its hammer until it fully locked. The sound of the hammer locking into position filled the sun-baked area. The lawman felt the inside of his mouth go dry as he took another few steps closer to the horseman. Gunn silently cursed the fact that the blinding sun was concealing the identity of the rider from his straining eyes.

Dust swirled around from where the sturdy horse had disturbed the soft ground. Gunn moved in front of the still unconscious Apache to protect him from any stray lead which might start flying at any moment.

The star rider raised his gun and held it at arm's length, aiming at the horseman.

'Who are ya?' Gunn bellowed out. 'Raise them arms or I'll kill ya. I ain't in no mood to take me no prisoners. Do ya hear me?'

The rider did not raise his arms. The sound of spurs filled the air as the horseman defiantly urged his mount to approach.

Gunn swallowed hard and wondered why his threat was being ignored. He gritted his teeth and frowned.

'I ain't joshing, stranger. I'll shoot if ya don't stop.'

9

'You would kill the great Zococa, *amigo*?' the smiling bandit asked as he guided his pinto stallion closer to the lawman. 'I have come many miles to see you and . . . '

Zococa did not finish his sentence. His eyes suddenly saw the motionless Tahoka propped against a saddle behind the star rider's legs. Gunn's eyes widened. He lowered his .45 as the horseman drew rein and carefully dismounted. The lawman accepted the long leathers as the bandit moved past him and knelt beside his friend. Gunn turned and looked down and saw the concern in the Mexican's face.

'I do not understand, *amigo*,' Zococa said. His hands tried to awaken his friend by moving Tahoka's head. 'What has happened to my little rhinoceros?'

Gunn held on to the reins of the

pinto. 'Some *hombre* shot him. I cut the bullet out and sewed him up.'

'So much blood,' the bandit noted.

'He'd spilled most of it before he showed up at the camp last night, Zococa,' Gunn said. 'I got me a feeling that he might not pull through.'

Zococa stood and narrowed his eyes. 'Tahoka will not die. He is very strong.'

The star rider nodded. 'Reckon he must be to have survived long enough to find me and Toby. I figure he was shot a couple of days back, coz most of the blood on his shirt was already dry when he got here.'

Zococa shook his head. 'Who would shoot Tahoka?'

'Maybe some critter reckoned if he shot Tahoka he might lead them to you,' Gunn suggested. 'There are a lot of folks who never believed that you were dead.'

'I am not dead, *amigo*,' the bandit said. He studied the area around them and saw the skillet close to the ashes of what had been a campfire. He moved across the sand, then carefully knelt and lifted the blackened skillet. His eyes stared at the bacon. 'What is this?'

'That was me and Toby's supper but we never got around to eating it,' Gunn answered. 'We got kinda busy when Tahoka showed up.'

'I do not blame you for not eating this.' Zococa turned, walked back to his friend and knelt again. He held the pan under the Apache's nose.

'What ya doing?'

Zococa briefly glanced at the star rider. 'Tahoka likes to eat, *amigo*. Maybe the smell of this burned bacon will awaken him from his sleep.'

'I surely doubt that.' The marshal shrugged. 'Me and Toby tried every damn thing we could think of to wake that critter up but nothing worked. That's why I'm feared he'll never open his eyes again.'

The bandit ignored the words of the lawman. 'He will wake.'

'How can ya be so sure?'

'I just know my little elephant is not ready to die just yet,' Zococa answered. 'You keep mentioning this Toby, but I see no one but us here. Where is he?'

'He rode out to go to my ranch and bring a wagon back,' Gunn explained. 'We figured that we would take Tahoka back there so he could heal up.'

Zococa nodded and moved the skillet back and forth beneath the Apache's nose. 'Wake up, Tahoka. We have to talk. We have to talk about why you left me at the church.'

'I thought ya was dead.' Gunn led the pinto stallion to the creek so that the magnificent animal could drink beside his own horse and that of Zococa's friend. 'Tahoka took ya to a church, huh?'

'Sí, amigo.' The bandit removed the bacon from the skillet and placed it against the unconscious warrior's mouth. The grease ran over the scarred lips of the Apache. 'Food. Eat, my little one. Eat and be strong.'

Gunn looped the reins of the pinto around the saddle horn of the Apache's mount and then strode back to the bandit.

'He might never wake up, ya know?'

'He will wake up,' Zococa insisted.

The marshal inhaled deeply and looked all about them. The hills to either side were well covered in trees of every known type. There was plenty of cover for anyone who might choose to bushwhack them, he thought.

'Who do ya figure it was that shot him, Zococa?'

The bandit looked at the star rider. 'Whoever it was did not do a very clever thing, *amigo*. He has hurt my little one and for that he will have to pay.'

Gunn tried to work out who might have shot the massive brave. Who and why?

'Do ya reckon it might have been another bandit?' Gunn suggested. 'A rival who thought ya was dead and he could kill Tahoka without paying the price?'

Zococa shook his head as he smeared the bacon all over the face of the

Apache. 'There are no bandits who would dare shoot the friend of the great Zococa, *amigo*. The people of Mexico would never hurt either of us.'

'What about Mexican lawmen?' Gunn bit his lip. 'There must be a few down south of the border who ain't feared of ya and would try and get their hands on the bounty you boys have on ya heads.'

'The only ones who are not afraid of me are dead.' The bandit stared down at his friend. 'I think there is only one type of rat who would shoot and try to kill Tahoka.'

'A stinking bounty hunter,' Hal Gunn heard himself say instinctively.

The Mexican bandit looked up at the star rider's face and could see the expression etched upon his weathered features. It was the same look he had first seen eighteen months earlier.

'I think you are right, *amigo*. I heard that there is one bounty hunter who has been hunting me and my little elephant for the longest time.' Zococa nodded to himself. 'His name is Crawford.'

Gunn knelt down beside the bandit. 'Did ya say Crawford?'

'*Sí, amigo.*'

'Hume Crawford?'

'That is the name many people have told to me,' Zococa said. 'I have heard he has killed many innocent people trying to find my trail. Maybe he thought if he killed Tahoka it might bring me out of hiding.'

Gunn nodded. 'Crawford is loco. I met him once and had to pay him bounty on a few outlaws he had killed. Every one of them outlaws had been shot in the back.'

Suddenly both men's attention was drawn to Tahoka. His eyes were open and he was licking his lips. The brave raised one of his arms, clawed the bacon from the skillet and swiftly devoured it.

'I told you that Tahoka would wake up.' Zococa beamed.

Hal Gunn nodded. Then something occurred to the star rider. It chilled him to the bone. He looked into the bandit's eyes.

'If Crawford is the one who shot Tahoka he must have trailed him across the border.' Gunn rubbed his mouth. 'He might have figured that Tahoka was going to ya. There's only one ranch around here and it belongs to me, Zococa. That crazy galoot might be heading to my ranch thinking he'll find you there. Ginny and Polly are there.'

'Do not be alarmed, *amigo*.' Zococa patted the troubled star rider's shoulder. 'This is a very big country. Crawford might not find your rancho.'

'Ya wrong, partner.' Gunn stood abruptly. 'Crawford knows where my ranch is. That's where he came with them dead outlaws after his bounty money. Damn it all. He might have decided that's where you are. Maybe he figured I had ya hidden there coz I owe ya a favour.'

The smile evaporated from the bandit's face. 'If you are right I do not think he will be very happy when he does not find me at your rancho, *amigo*.'

Gunn clenched his fists. 'We have to ride.'

'Are your lovely angels alone on the rancho, *amigo*?'

'Nope. I've got two ranch hands there but they've never tangled with anyone like Hume Crawford before.'

'*Sí*. Crawford does not take prisoners,' Zococa added.

'We gotta ride now,' Gunn said urgently.

Zococa tossed the skillet aside and stood up next to the troubled lawman. 'No, *amigo*. It is Zococa who has to ride. You will take care of my little elephant until he is strong enough to follow us.'

'But that crazy backshooter might kill my family.'

'No one will hurt your golden-haired angels.' Zococa turned on his heel and, defying his own pain, ran to the pinto stallion. He tore his reins free and mounted the high-shouldered animal. 'This I promise you, *amigo*. And as I have told you before, legends never break their promises.'

141

Gunn could not believe his eyes as he watched the intrepid horseman spur his mount and thunder up through the trees. The lawman looked down at Tahoka. The Apache warrior touched his chest with his hand and nodded his noble head. It was his way of thanking the man he knew had saved his life.

'Can ya ride, Tahoka?'

The large, silent man forced his massive frame off the sand and rested a hand on the star rider's shoulder. For a moment he did not move, then he walked slowly towards his mount.

Gunn hauled his saddle off the sand and raced to his own horse. He threw the hefty saddle over the blanket on the animal's back and secured its cinch strap.

Somehow the Apache warrior managed to mount his horse. He sat astride the rested gelding as he watched the star rider throw himself on to his own horse.

'Are ya ready, old friend?' Gunn asked.

Tahoka gave a slow nod. Both horsemen started for the distant ranch.

10

The pinto stallion thundered up through the brush with its intrepid master standing high in his stirrups. It was a trail the bandit knew well. There were few men on either side of the law who could ride unhindered and unseen through a mainly barren land.

But Zococa had every short cut branded into his memory. It had served him well. He did not ride the trails created by others, for that would have proved suicidal for a man who had been wanted dead or alive for nearly a third of his short life.

Zococa had worked out long ago that all the trails that linked one remote settlement to another had been made by those who used wagons or stagecoaches.

A horseman was never restricted by the width of a well-used trail for he could travel anywhere as long as it was wide enough for his mount to negoti-ate.

The bandit galloped over the top of the high mountain rise then dragged his reins up to his chest as he looked all around him. He was not trying to get his bearings but was looking to see if there were any other riders heading in the same direction as himself.

There was.

Far down to his right Zococa caught sight of hoof dust rising up from beyond the dry brush. The fertile mind of the young horseman remembered that Gunn had sent his deputy to his ranch by way of the old wagon road. Zococa instantly knew that it must be the deputy.

He turned his mount. His eyes were seeking another rider. A more ruthless breed of horseman who, he feared, might be ahead of him.

His entire body was suddenly racked by pain.

The bandit was in agony. His savage injuries still dogged him even though he would never admit it, for to do so was to be mortal like other men. He had ridden a long way from San Remo and knew that his journey was far from over. He could see that the distant sun was now on its path down towards the far-off horizon yet, with his far superior knowledge of the terrain, Zococa was confident that he would reach the ranch a long time before Toby Jones managed the feat.

He gritted his teeth and continued to search for any sign of the bounty hunter. He prayed that he was wrong and that Crawford was not heading for Gunn's ranch, but every ounce of the slim bandit knew that this time he was correct. Zococa had not told the already troubled marshal that as soon as he had crossed the border he had discovered the dead body of an old man in a ramshackle cabin.

The senseless killing bore all the hallmarks of the deranged bounty hunter. Crawford considered himself above the law and that made him far more dangerous than most men of his profession.

With the intensity of an eagle Zococa studied everything from his high vantage point. Nothing was dismissed out of hand.

Set about ten miles from where he steadied his magnificent pinto stallion the ranch belonging to the star rider and what remained of his family was bathed in the blazing rays of the sun. Zococa could see the newly built structures which replaced the ones burned down by the Comancheros. The half-built wooden framework of a barn stood near the site of its predecessor.

Zococa was about to spur on when something else caught his attention far to his left. The bandit turned his mount, lowered the brim of his black sombrero against the sun and narrowed his eyes.

The bandit stared intently from the high ridge towards a place where trees and wild brush covered the rolling hills. There seemed to be nothing to see but his honed instincts told him that someone was moving through the dry woodland.

He had seen something from the corner of his eye, but what?

Zococa held his reins in his hands and kept watching for what felt like a lifetime. Then, as he was about to turn away and continue on towards the ranch, he saw a vague whisper of dust.

It was barely visible above the tops of the trees as it drifted up into the cloudless blue sky, but Zococa saw it. His unrivalled survival instinct had not deserted him. He knew that a mere whisper of dust might not have been noticed by anyone else, but to him it told a story.

It warned of a devilish tale of impending death.

More dust floated up through the trees. This time it was even nearer to Hal Gunn's remote cattle ranch. Something inside Zococa told him that it was the same man who had shot Tahoka and killed so many others in his insane attempt to find him.

It must be Crawford, Zococa thought. His narrowed eyes darted from the telltale dust back to the ranch. He tried to calculate who was closest to the home of the little golden angel. Was it the unseen horseman or was it himself?

It was an even bet who would reach the ranch first.

Then, as he adjusted his aching body on the high-shouldered pinto stallion, Zococa remembered his strange dream. The dream which had made him leave the safety of San Remo to return to a place he had last visited eighteen long months previously.

He remembered the small, beautiful face of the golden-haired angel who lived there. The small child named Polly had visited him in a dream and seemed to be calling out for him to fulfil his promise and return. Zococa had known many beautiful women in his life but none of them had stolen his heart the way she had. It was if she had blessed him with a reason not to die.

His hands hauled his reins to his right. He turned the handsome pinto and guided it down through the trees

148

until the land grew more level.

A sudden urgency overwhelmed the bandit as dust and debris flew up from the hoofs of the stallion. Zococa spurred and thundered through the trees. Now it was a race against time and the deadly killer who, he knew, was getting closer and closer to Gunn's cattle spread with every beat of his pounding heart.

The Mexican bandit rose in his stirrups and allowed his mount to find its full pace.

'Fly, my handsome one,' Zococa called out to his galloping stallion beneath him. 'Fly like the wind.'

11

The cloudless sky above the ranch had turned the colour of fresh blood. The heavens were on fire. It was an omen which Virginia recognized as she stood by her kitchen window and looked out at the sun's last embers. For hours she had sensed something was wrong and yet she could not work out what. Unknown to Virginia Gunn there were two horsemen galloping towards the heart of the ranch, one with evil intent whilst the other was willing to sacrifice his life in order to stop the insane bounty hunter.

Virginia still could not explain why she felt so uneasy.

Both her ranch hands were sitting on the porch outside the bunkhouse. Both had their guns on their hips. The men were within spitting distance of the larger building and were ready to tackle anything that might happen their way.

Virginia walked away from the window and pushed a strand of loose golden hair back behind her ear as she moved towards her daughter. Little Polly was sitting on the stone hearth of the fireplace, playing with her dolls. The child looked up at her mother.

'The cookies are cold now, Mommy,' she announced. 'Ya said Pa would be home soon. Now we're gonna have to make more.'

Virginia knelt and ran her hand over her daughter's head. She smiled and gave a nod of agreement.

'I think that ya right, sweetheart,' Virginia said.

Polly frowned. Her lower lip quivered as if she were about to burst into tears. 'He's OK, ain't he?'

Virginia took hold of Polly and hugged her. 'Sure he is, honey. I bet him and Toby just ran into a little trouble. Some folks break the law and they have to be spanked.'

The child looked up into her mother's face. 'Mommy, don't ya know anything? They don't spank bad men. They chase them away.'

Before Virginia could respond she heard Rex and Billy raise their voices. Both men sounded irate. She stood and started towards the door.

'Stay here, Polly.'

As usual the small girl did not listen. She trailed her mother to the door and watched as the bolt was slid across. Virginia opened it and stepped out into the strange, reddish light.

'What's wrong?' Virginia asked the hands.

Rex pointed in one direction as Billy aimed his drawn gun in another. Virginia looked to both the places the men were looking at.

'We got two riders headed here, Ginny,' Billy said.

'Maybe it's Hal and Toby,' the woman suggested as she felt her daughter's hands clutching her long dress.

Rex shook his head. 'From two different directions? I sure doubt that, ma'am.'

Virginia realized the men were jumpy.

She had never seen them like that before and it worried her more than the thought of the two unknown riders. Her eyes darted from one of the approaching horsemen to the other. It was impossible to make out either of them clearly. They were at least a mile apart and both were riding hard towards the centre of the ranch courtyard. Dust was spiralling up into the crimson sky from both mounts.

'Any notion who they are?' she asked.

Billy moved closer to her as he too kept looking from one rider to the other. 'I don't know who either of them are, Ginny, but I reckon ya best take Polly inside and bolt the door and windows, though.'

She gave a worried nod. 'I think ya right.'

Virginia turned round and ushered her daughter into the house. She closed the door behind them.

No sooner had the two cowboys heard the door's bolt being secured than Crawford suddenly opened up with his long-barrelled Winchester as his grey mount thundered closer and closer towards them.

Large chunks of wood were torn from the side of the bunkhouse wall as bullets cut through the air from the bounty hunter's rifle. The two cowboys crouched down as they heard each of the ranch house's wooden window shutters being secured behind them.

'Holy cow. That critter's shooting at us,' Rex said. He dropped on to the ground beside the bunkhouse porch. He cocked his .45 and fired over and over again.

As another volley of bullets tore even more wood from the wall, Billy rested his back against it. 'Stop wasting bullets, Rex. We ain't got the range with these six-shooters.'

Rex spat out dust. 'How come his bullets are chewing up our woodwork?'

'He's using a damn carbine,' Billy replied. He watched the horseman galloping through the scarlet hues of the sinking sun. 'Most likely one of them new-fangled Winchesters I heard about.

They say they can hold sixteen bullets under the extra-long barrel.'

Rex pushed himself up off the sand and stepped on to the raised porch. 'I'll get our scatterguns. If he gets close enough we can make soup out of him and his damn horse.'

Billy turned his gun round the wall and fired. 'Good thinking. If he gets close enough and we're still alive we can blast him to hell.'

Rex raced into the bunkhouse. He did not take long to rustle up their shotguns and two boxes of ammunition. The cowboy came cautiously back out and slid a scattergun and a box of large cartridges to his pal. Then he recalled the other horseman heading towards them from the opposite direction. Rex turned round, moved along the porch and screwed up his eyes.

'The other varmint ain't shooting, Billy,' Rex said as he forced two shells into the big scattergun. He pulled the hefty double barrels up until they snapped shut.

'Who do ya figure they are?' Billy called out as another half-dozen rifle shots rang out and peppered the side wall of the bunkhouse. A cloud of smouldering sawdust showered over the cowboy.

'Whoever that'un is I reckon he don't like us.' Rex wondered if he ought to fire at the other horseman. Yet he had been taught by Hal Gunn never to fire first, for you often ended up killing the wrong man. 'Do ya reckon I ought to shoot at this varmint, Billy? He ain't fired at us.'

'Hold ya fire on him,' Billy said as he stared at the bounty hunter. 'We got us enough trouble with this gun-happy bastard.'

Rex rested the hefty weapon against the wall and drew his Colt again. As he looked up he could no longer see the second rider. The approaching Zococa had seemingly vanished.

'He's gone, Billy,' the cowboy gasped. 'Where'd he go?'

'What?' Billy ran to his pal's side.

Billy looked troubled. 'He must have headed behind the house. Don't pay him no mind. Get here and help me fend off this'un.'

'Do ya figure they're working together?' Rex trailed back to Billy at the corner of the bunkhouse, where half of the wall had been shot up. Blackened scars covered its surface.

Before Billy could reply another volley of rifle bullets cut through the corner of the wall. Billy arched as sawdust engulfed him. Rex shook his head as he felt the hot splinters fill his eyes. He rubbed his face and then saw his pal stagger and fall from the porch. Two of the bullets had hit the cowboy in his side. Blood spread out from his motionless body.

'Billy?' Rex gasped. 'Are ya OK?'

There was no reply.

Then the stunned cowboy heard the hoofs of the grey stallion echoing off the wooden buildings all around the courtyard. Rex knelt in the cloud of choking sawdust and cocked the hammer of his gun. Then the grey stallion burst out of the dust and gunsmoke, right beside him.

The startled cowboy raised and wildly fired his six-shooter just as Hume Crawford squeezed the trigger of his Winchester. The rifle bullet went clean through the cowboy. A gaping hole in Rex's back spewed gore all over the porch. The half-dead cowboy vainly tried to claw the hammer of his .45 back again. Crawford fired another lethally accurate shot and watched as Rex toppled, lifeless, on to his side. A sickening gasp escaped from his mouth.

With cold-blooded efficiency the bounty hunter had killed both of the ranch's defenders. Hume Crawford rammed his smoking rifle into its saddle scabbard and pulled both his guns from his gunbelt. The bounty hunter looped a leg over the neck of his grey as he slid to the ground.

There was still one more notch to add to his tally. Zococa had yet to be killed.

His eyes burned into the ranch house

as the sun finally set and the entire area was bathed in the strange half-light that always came between sundown and the appearance of the first of the stars.

Zococa had seen the unmistakable flashes of gunfire as he had vainly attempted to reach the heart of the ranch before the bounty hunter. He had seen the cowboy's gun glinting in the last crimson rays of the sun and decided that it was far wiser to ride around the rear of the large ranch house than to risk being shot by accident.

The young bandit hauled rein and dismounted from the pinto. He stroked the animal's neck.

'You did good, my handsome one,' Zococa told the animal as he tied its reins to a dead tree stump. 'Remain here until I return.'

Zococa was in pain. He could feel every one of his stitched-up bullet holes as he strode through the brush towards the rear of the long house. The scars felt like red-hot pokers being thrust into him. His skin seemed no longer to fit him as it had once done.

The bandit paused as he realized that the shooting had abruptly ended. That meant only one thing, Zococa told himself. Both the cowboys must be dead.

Cowboys were no match for someone who lived by the gun.

Crawford might have been insane but he was a deadly marksman, even though he usually tended to shoot either unarmed people or those who had their backs turned to his gun barrels.

The bandit pulled his silver pistol from its holster on his left hip and hastily checked it was fully loaded. He then dropped the weapon back into the leather and moved forward.

Zococa reached the rear wall of the house. He glanced along its length. Marshal Gunn had not built any windows at the back of his house but he had built a rear door.

He moved towards the door.

Inside the besieged ranch house,

Virginia Gunn held her daughter to her bosom and prayed as she had only prayed once before. She too realized why the shooting had come to such an abrupt halt.

The interior of the house was in darkness.

The two bedrooms were next to one another at the far end of the building. Both had windows that faced east. Both windows, like all of the others, were shuttered and locked.

Virginia held Polly tightly under the table, which still had two plates of cookies upon it. Her lips were against the child's right ear.

'Quiet, honey,' she whispered.

Then outside the front door both mother and daughter heard the sound of spurs as Crawford stepped up on to the porch. The spurs rang out as the bounty hunter paced along the raised wooden walkway. Virginia heard the shutter over the kitchen window rattle as it was tested.

'What was that, Mommy?'

'Nothing, Polly.'

The long strides of the lethal bounty hunter started back towards the door. His spurs jangled with every step. Then the door began to rock on its hinges as it too was tested.

'Someone is out there, Mommy.'

Virginia held her daughter even tighter. 'Your pa will be home soon. Don't go worrying.'

Polly looked up at her mother. 'Are we going to die?'

Before Virginia could answer her daughter, the voice of Zococa filled both their ears with his familiar hushed tones.

'Angels cannot die, my beautiful one,' the bandit said as he entered the house and carefully closed the rear door behind him. Both stared in disbelief from under the table at the still handsome bandit clad entirely in black. 'Do not fret. I am here to protect you.'

'Zococa.' Polly beamed.

'How did you get in?' Virginia asked. 'I bolted that door.'

The bandit walked past them and stared at the more sturdy front door. 'There are no doors that can stop the son of the greatest lock picker in all of Mexico, dear lady.'

'Why are ya here?' Virginia whispered.

'I had a dream,' Zococa replied.

'Just like me,' Polly smiled.

'I don't understand,' Virginia said.

The bandit shrugged. 'To tell the truth, neither do I.'

The door suddenly rocked as Crawford hammered the grips of both his six-shooters against it. The bandit did not flinch.

'I know ya hiding in there, Zococa,' Crawford's voice boomed out. 'That stinking marshal got ya hid just coz ya helped him save his womenfolk.'

Zococa raised an eyebrow and leaned over the table. He smiled at the woman and child hidden beneath it. 'Lock the door after I leave. Then get back under the table. Stay there and do not come out until I tell you it is safe.'

Polly and her mother watched as the

163

bandit headed back to the rear door and disappeared out into the night air. Virginia crawled out from under the table and raced to the door. She slid the bolt across it and returned to Polly.

They huddled together and continued to pray.

★ ★ ★

In the few minutes between Zococa's entering and leaving the ranch house it had gone dark. The moon was still low and as yet its eerie light had not yet reached the centre of the cattle spread. The bandit walked slowly round the house through the dark shadows. He made no noise. His steps were not betrayed by the spurs worn by so many other horsemen. His spurs were silent.

The bandit tightened the drawstring of his black sombrero under his chin as he came round the corner of the long-fronted house. He stopped and stared through the ghostly light at the horrific scene before him.

Both the cowboys lay in their own gore where they had fallen. Zococa then diverted his eyes to the bounty hunter. He had never seen the man but instantly he knew it was the devilish Crawford. There had been so many detailed stories about the creature who killed the innocent to get to wanted men with bounty on their heads that Zococa knew whom he was staring at.

Zococa watched as the bounty hunter kept pounding his guns on the door. Then he began his approach.

'You seek me, *señor*?' the bandit asked.

Crawford turned on his heel in stunned shock. He glared at the bandit. It was like a hungry man looking at a banquet as he slowly recognized the elegant figure before him.

'Zococa?' the bounty hunter asked, his thumbs eagerly pulling back on his gun hammers.

'*Sí*,' Zococa replied. 'And you are Crawford the hunter of men?'

'Ya know me?' The bounty hunter was surprised.

Zococa nodded.

'I'm gonna kill ya, boy,' Crawford said as he slowly turned his guns on his prey.

'Tell me, *amigo*,' Zococa said, 'do you believe in God?'

Crawford spat, raised his weapons and growled, 'Nope.'

Both the bounty hunter's guns blasted. Two hot tapers of deadly venom sped along the porch. Zococa moved behind one of its uprights and drew his pistol. He fanned the gun hammer once and saw Crawford knocked off his feet. The body landed heavily on the boards. Crawford's arms fell limply to his sides and the guns fell from his hands. The legendary speed of his ability to draw and fire his pistol had not deserted the bandit. Neither had his accuracy.

Yet Zococa felt no satisfaction. He slid the gun back into its holster, walked towards the body and paused.

He stared down at his handiwork and sighed.

'It is a shame you did not believe in God, *amigo*,' the bandit said. 'Now you have nowhere to go but to the bowels of Hell.'

Finale

The memory of the last shot which had been fired still hung in the evening air as the deputy rode up towards the remote ranch house. The acrid aroma of fresh gunsmoke filled his nostrils as he steadied his mount. Toby Jones had never been as frightened as he was now, as his gloved hands steered his lathered-up horse through the smoke, past the bunkhouse. There had been a battle here, he told himself. He had heard the shooting when he had still been a few miles up the road. Now he was witnessing what each of those shots had meant. His eyes looked at the bullet-ridden buildings. Then he stared at the three dead bodies and jerked his reins up to his tin star. The horse stopped and snorted as the smell of blood filled the animal's nostrils. Toby dismounted and nervously drew his gun.

He moved cautiously to the side of

the bunkhouse and rested a gloved hand on the shattered woodwork. Bullets had torn nearly half the wall away. The deputy glanced down and recognized the body closest to him. It was Billy. He gasped and clutched his six-shooter even tighter. Then as he moved forward towards the main house he saw Rex.

'What happened here?' Toby muttered as he defied his own fear and continued on towards the third body lying on the porch a few feet from the door. He wanted to turn and run but he knew that he had to find out whether Gunn's wife and daughter had escaped this slaughter. He stepped up on to the boardwalk of the long porch and screwed up his eyes.

He did not know the third body. There was a marked difference between this one and the cowboys, he thought. This man had been killed cleanly. One deadly accurate bullet had ended this man's existence. Toby summoned his inner strength and looked at the door.

'Are ya OK, Ginny?' Toby Jones called out. 'Are you and Polly OK?'

A voice came from inside the house. 'Is that you, Toby?'

'Yes, ma'am.'

The door swung open. Lamplight glowed upon the nervous deputy. Virginia looked at him. 'We're fine. Where's Hal, Toby?'

The confused young lawman walked towards the woman. 'What happened here, ma'am?'

'Where's my husband?' she repeated as he slid his gun back into its holster. 'Where's Hal? Is he OK? Why ain't he with you?'

'He's fine. He's down the road.' The deputy had only just answered when the attention of both was drawn to the trail down from the wagon road. They looked and saw the two approaching horses. Gunn and Tahoka rode into the courtyard and stopped their mounts by the porch steps.

'Hal.' Virginia sighed heavily as a sudden wave of relief enveloped her.

'Are you and Polly OK, Ginny darling?'
She nodded. 'We're fine.'

The star rider slid from his horse and helped the wounded Apache warrior down to the ground. They mounted the steps to where the deputy and the smiling Virginia stood. Gunn looked along the porch at Crawford's body. He then glanced at his dead cowboys and shook his head sadly.

Gunn hugged his wife before lifting her off her feet and kissing her. She was blushing when he lowered her down again.

'Damn, I missed ya,' Gunn whispered into her ear. 'I ain't ever leaving you gals again. Me and Toby are gonna quit being star riders. We're gonna protect you. Nothing like this will ever happen again. I promise ya.'

Virginia's eyes filled with tears. 'Thank God.'

Gunn looked at his wife. 'Where's Zococa, Ginny? He's gotta be here. Only he could have stopped that evil bounty hunter with one shot.'

Virginia pointed into the ranch house. The famed bandit was sitting on the hearth in front of the fireplace as the little girl played happily at his feet.

Tahoka brushed past the female and the star riders. He walked into the room, and stared down at his old friend and started to talk with his hands to the bandit.

Zococa looked at the warrior and grinned.

'I am fine, my little elephant.' He sighed and waved his finger at the huge brave. 'Do not worry. This time I did not get shot, unlike you.'

Tahoka snorted and made his way to the kitchen table. He sat down and started to consume the cookies.

Polly suddenly noticed her father and ran to him. He hoisted her into the air and hugged her.

'I missed ya, Pa,' Polly said.

'I'm never leaving the ranch again, Polly,' Gunn vowed.

Zococa got to his feet as the star riders and Virginia walked towards him.

His grin lit up the room.

'Ya saved my gals' lives again, old friend,' Gunn said to the bandit. 'I can never repay ya. What in tarnation brought ya here?'

Zococa touched the long hair of the child in the star rider's powerful arms. He smiled wistfully.

'A little golden-haired angel brought me here, *amigo*.'

THE END

We do hope that you have enjoyed reading this large print book.

Did you know that all of our titles are available for purchase?

We publish a wide range of high quality large print books including:
Romances, Mysteries, Classics
General Fiction
Non Fiction and Westerns

Special interest titles available in large print are:
The Little Oxford Dictionary
Music Book, Song Book
Hymn Book, Service Book

Also available from us courtesy of Oxford University Press:
Young Readers' Dictionary
(large print edition)
Young Readers' Thesaurus
(large print edition)

For further information or a free brochure, please contact us at:
Ulverscroft Large Print Books Ltd.,
The Green, Bradgate Road, Anstey,
Leicester, LE7 7FU, England.
Tel: (00 44) **0116 236 4325**
Fax: (00 44) **0116 234 0205**

DARROW'S GAMBLE

Gillian F. Taylor

'Set a thief to catch a thief!' It's a risky strategy for a lawman to take, but Sheriff Darrow has very personal reasons for wanting to catch bank robber Tom Croucher. Forced to stay in Wyoming, Darrow is relying on two convicted criminals, Tomcat Billy and Irish, to do the job for him. But Tomcat hates Darrow, while Irish wants to go straight. They join Croucher's gang, but who deserves their loyalty — the outlaw or the sheriff?

DALTON AND THE SUNDOWN KID

Ed Law

When Dalton rides into Lonetree looking for work, he finds a town crippled by the local outlaw — the Sundown Kid. Tasked with resolving the Kid's latest kidnapping, Dalton must deliver a ransom to the bandit to secure the safe return of young Sera. Culver. However, before he reaches the rendezvous point, the ransom is stolen. Then a fearsome shootout leaves him stranded in the wilderness . . . With the fate of a woman at stake, can Dalton fight the good fight and prevail?